Praise for
THE BOYS START THE WAR

'Sure to be a hit with children who want an easy read spiked with chuckles and chortles. Nifty Naylor nails 'em again!"
—*School Library Journal*

'A rambunctious tale of an age-old feud between two ancient clans: the boys and the girls."
—*The Bulletin of the Center for Children's Books*

'Packed with action. . . . Newbery winner Naylor blends her ingredients in typically deft fashion . . . helps create another crowd-pleaser."
—*Publishers Weekly*

PHYLLIS REYNOLDS NAYLOR

THE BOYS START THE WAR

SCHOLASTIC INC.

New York Toronto London Auckland Sydney
Mexico City New Delhi Hong Kong Buenos Aires

*To the young readers of Buckhannon, West Virginia,
which is almost, but not quite,
the location of this story.*

ISBN 0-439-89403-4

Copyright © 1993 by Phyllis Reynolds Naylor.
All rights reserved. Published by Scholastic Inc., 557 Broadway,
New York, NY 10012, by arrangement with Random House
Children's Books, a division of Random House, Inc.
SCHOLASTIC and associated logos are trademarks
and/or registered trademarks of Scholastic Inc.

12 11   10 11/0

Printed in the U.S.A.   40

First Scholastic printing, October 2006

Contents

▼

One

▼

The Aliens

"The island's sinking!"

Wally studied the rivers of yellow that began streaming out from the middle.

"Sandbags! Sandbags!" he cried, lifting his waffle up at the edges with his fork, first one side, then the other.

If he made a little cut in each corner, the hot syrup traveled from one square to the next, but if he poured the syrup directly over the pat of butter, sitting like an island in the middle of his breakfast, the island grew smaller and smaller as the butter melted, until finally . . .

"They're coming!"

The back door banged and Wally jumped. Jake and Josh came tumbling into the kitchen, followed by seven-year-old Peter.

"Who?" asked Wally.

"The new guys over in Bensons' house!" Jake

1

grabbed the field glasses from the shelf where Mother kept them after she finished her bird-watching. "C'mon!"

Feet pounded on the stairs, and Wally knew that his brothers were headed for the trapdoor in the attic ceiling and the small balcony on top of the house—the widow's walk, it was called—where they could see out over the whole town, practically.

He sighed, picked up his plate and fork, and went up the first flight of stairs to the bedrooms, then the second set of stairs to the attic.

He could never understand why his two older brothers were always in such a rush. Sooner or later they would find out whether the three new boys in that family were their own ages or not, so why the hurry? Wally felt that you should spend the last week of summer vacation as lazily as possible, and now he couldn't even enjoy his waffle in peace.

Yesterday Josh had been sitting under a tree sketching Martians, or what he thought Martians would look like. Jake had been figuring out what they would all do on Halloween, and Wally and Peter had been lying in the grass, watching ants crawling in and out of a rotten apple—exactly the kinds of ways you expected to spend a summer day. Peter was the only one in the family who liked to study things the way Wally did. They both had brown hair, blue eyes, and thick, sturdy hands like their father's. Jake and Josh, however, were string-bean skinny, with skin that tanned by the first week of June.

Jake already had the stepladder in place, and Josh climbed to the top and pushed up on the trapdoor. Blue sky shone through the square opening as a shower of pigeon droppings rained down on them. One piece landed on Wally's waffle. One gray-white blob of digested worms and bugs. Wally stared helplessly at his plate, then set it on the floor and followed his brothers to the balcony above.

He sat down in one corner and watched as Jake inched forward on his stomach, field glasses in hand, until he was close to the railing. The wind whipped at Wally's shirt, but it was a warm, dry wind that spelled September.

"Why are they just sitting there?" Jake wondered aloud, holding the glasses steady as he stared across the river.

Wally squinted, studying the car in the driveway of the house at the end of Island Avenue. The large piece of land in the middle of Buckman was not really an island, because water surrounded only three sides of it, but people called it "The Island" anyway. If you were coming in from the east, you entered Buckman on Island Avenue and kept going until you were out on the very tip, and then you crossed the bridge over into the business district. You might not even have noticed that the river on your right was the same as that on your left; it simply looped about at the end of the island.

"Okay, a door's opening, here they come!" said Jake.

"How old are they?" Josh asked.

Wally hoped there would be friends for each of them—an eleven-year-old for the twins, a nine-year-old for him, and a seven-year-old friend for Peter. The family that had moved out of the house on the other side of the river—who had left West Virginia to go to Georgia—had five boys of all ages, and they had been the best friends the Hatfords ever had.

"Well, say something!" demanded Peter when Jake didn't answer. "Are they aliens or what?"

"There's the father," said Jake. "Now someone's getting out one of the back doors. . . . A guy about twelve, I'd guess. . . ."

"Yea!" cheered Josh.

"No, wait a minute . . . it's a girl . . . no, a boy. . . ." Jake's voice began to fade. "A girl. She just took off her cap."

A girl! Wally and Josh stared at each other. Who said anything about girls?

Josh took the field glasses next. He sat with his elbows propped on his knees, staring across the river. "No one else is getting out. . . . Now the other door's opening. It's the mother. . . . Here come the rest." He gasped. "Another girl . . . !"

"*Two* girls?" wailed Jake.

Wally thoughtfully bit his lip. This *was* serious! He grabbed the field glasses himself. "My turn," he said.

At the tip of the island a man and woman stood looking up at a large old house. Wally could see a

4

tall girl behind them, leaning against a tree and holding a baseball cap in one hand. A smaller girl was running down to the river.

Another leg emerged from the backseat of the car. A sneakered foot, faded jeans, a knee, a thigh, and then the last member of the new family got out and stretched.

"A girl," said Wally, disbelieving, and handed the field glasses back to Josh.

Nobody spoke for almost a minute.

"They're aliens, all right," said Josh.

"Three kids in one family and they're all girls?" Jake cried incredulously. "I thought Mrs. Benson told Mom they had rented their house to a family with three boys!"

Wally tried to remember exactly. "She said she thought there were three kids—"

"And that maybe we would still have enough to play baseball. . . ." added Josh. "*I* thought she meant *boys*!"

Wally's shoulders slumped. For years, ever since he could remember, the Hatford and Benson boys had got together every afternoon, rain or shine, to shoot BBs, fish, swim, play kick-the-can, camp out near Smuggler's Cove, climb Knob Hill, explore the old coal mine, or just lie on their backs in the grass and talk.

More than that, with the five Benson boys, the Hatford brothers regularly won first place in the costume contest at Halloween. One year they had each dressed up like some of the teachers at school; another year they had been dominoes; and a third year they chained themselves together like a prison gang. With the nine of them they had their own baseball team, and every May played a team from Grafton. They had even started their own band. Nothing would be the same again.

Wally stared out over the hills that dipped and rose like a roller coaster all around Buckman. The steeples of the United Methodist Church and the college chapel peeped up over the tops of the trees surrounding the courthouse, and the shiny horseshoe of a river curved around the island. It was a wonderful old town, but anytime he and his brothers walked over the swinging footbridge now, they would find three girls in the last house on Island Avenue, not the friends they had known all their lives.

"We just figured it would be a family of boys, that's all," he said at last.

"Well, we figured wrong," said Josh.

For a long while there was not another sound from the widow's walk. Finally Jake broke the silence:

"Let's burn the bridge."

Wally turned and stared. "What?"

"Just go down there some night and burn the footbridge," Jake said. "Then the girls couldn't get over to our side of the river. Not here, anyway.

They'd have to cross the road bridge and get to school the long way around."

"Don't be dumb," said Josh. "Dad would kill us."

"We don't have to burn the bridge. We'll just never invite them over here," said Wally.

"That's not enough," said Jake.

"We won't have anything to do with them," offered his twin, whose arms and legs were as long and spidery as Jake's.

"Not enough," said Jake.

"Well, what *do* you want to do, then? Vaporize them?" asked Peter, getting right to the point.

Jake sat with his lips pressed hard together and Wally could almost see currents connecting in his brain. Jake was the ringleader, the planner, and he usually got his way. "Do you remember the movie we saw once, *The Gang from Reno*?"

"Yeah," said Josh and Wally.

"No," said Peter.

"It was about this village up in the mountains," Jake told him. "A motorcycle gang from Reno comes and takes over. But the villagers finally drive them out just by making them miserable. We've got to make the new people miserable."

Wally leaned against the railing and studied Jake. It sounded pretty awful, even talking about it. "How do you know that the Bensons will move back if we do?"

"Because they weren't sure they'd like Georgia,

so they're only renting out their house here instead of selling. If they have trouble keeping renters, they just might give up and move back. You *know* they'd really rather live here. *Any*body would rather live here. We're just helping them make up their minds, that's all."

"But how are we going to make the new family miserable?" asked Josh, and they all turned to Wally. This always happened. Wally got involved whether he wanted to or not. He always said the first thing that came to his head, and that's why his brothers asked him.

"*Think*, Wally!" said Jake. "Think of the most terrible, awful, disgusting, horrible thing in the world."

Wally tried. He wondered if there was anything more awful or disgusting than pigeon poop on a waffle.

"Dead fish," he said finally.

Jake and Josh looked at each other.

"That's it!" yelped Josh. "We could dump them on the bank over on the other side, and the family will think the river's polluted."

"We'll dump everything dead we can find, and they'll be afraid to swim or fish or anything," said Jake. "Start collecting all the dead stuff you can, and put it in a bag in the garage. Great idea, Wally!"

"Hoo boy!" cried Josh. "The war is on!"

"Wow!" said Peter.

Wally blinked. How had this happened? What

had become of his wonderful day? Only a few minutes ago he'd been peacefully planning to float a waffle box down the river—see if it would make the curve at the end of Island Avenue and come back up the other side. Then he was going to climb to the top of the courthouse to see if there really were bats up there, the way Josh said, and after that he was going to jump from the largest branch of the sycamore into the river, and maybe he would even have gone out to the cemetery after dark, just to say he'd been.

He waited his turn at the trapdoor and slowly climbed down the ladder to the attic below. He picked up his plate, went down to the kitchen, scrunched up the empty waffle box and his waffle along with it, and then, with a sigh, threw them both in the trash.

Two

▼

Burial at Sea

Caroline Malloy leapt out of the car and rushed across the lawn, her ponytail flying out behind her like a flag.

"The river!" she screeched. "Beth! Eddie! Look!"

Edith Ann, the oldest, who hated her name and made everyone call her Eddie, stuck her baseball cap back on her head and wandered over. Beth, who had had her nose in a book, *The Living Tentacles of Planet Z*, ever since the family left Ohio that morning, came slowly across the yard, turning a page as she walked, and probably would have stepped right off the edge of the bank if Caroline hadn't caught her.

"Look!" Caroline said again, and the three sisters stared out over the Buckman River.

They were lined up like steps. Eddie, eleven, was tallest by far, and always wore her cap, even to the dinner table. Beth, ten, was fair-haired and pale-skinned, and tended to list to one side in a strong wind. It was eight-year-old Caroline, with dark hair and eyes like her father's, who had big plans for that river. Caroline, her mother always said, was precocious.

"I hope there are rapids!" she cried. "I hope there's a dam and a waterfall and quicksand and snakes . . ."

She couldn't go on. It was just too exciting. If they were only going to be here a year, she wanted to make the most of it. Caroline wanted to be an actress, and she imagined a scene in which she was floating unconscious in the water, heading for the falls, and someone had to rescue her. Or she might be sinking in quicksand, and would cleverly grab a vine at the last minute to pull herself out.

If it was a really dangerous scene where she had to paddle through rapids or something, she could always count on Eddie to be her stuntwoman. In fact, if Eddie did the hard parts and Beth wrote the script, the three of them could play almost any scene they liked.

They'd call their company Malloy Studios, her dream went on, and it would take its place beside Universal and Paramount in Hollywood. Actress, scriptwriter, and stuntwoman, all related. Not that Beth and Eddie knew anything about this, of course.

"*Caroline on the River,*" she said to the others. "Would that make a good movie title, Beth?"

"The River on Caroline, maybe," Eddie told her.

Beth made a face. "Movie titles have to be mysterious, like *Faces in the Water* or *Curses in the Current* or something."

"How about *The Nymph from Nowhere?*" Caroline suggested. "How does that sound?"

"Girls!" yelled their father. "We need your help unloading before the van gets here. I've got to move the car."

Caroline took one last look over her shoulder as she followed her sisters back to the house. Picking up her own suitcase, she went upstairs, where Eddie and Beth were choosing bedrooms. She didn't much care what room she had, because as far as she was concerned, there was only one place she really belonged, and that was onstage. *Some*where in her life there was a stage, a camera, lights, and a script just for her.

"You can have this room, Caroline," Eddie said, showing her the one next to the bath.

Caroline dropped her things on the floor and went right to the window to study the river once again, Eddie leaning over her shoulder.

"Hey!" Eddie said after a moment. "Look over there!"

"Where?"

"On top of that house across the river. Do you see something moving?"

Caroline rested her chin on her hands and

squinted. She *did* see something, but she wasn't sure what.

"I'll get Dad's binoculars," she said, running downstairs and out to the car.

"Take something with you as you go," her father insisted as she started toward the house again, and Caroline picked up a bag filled with shoes.

When she returned, Beth was in her room also.

"What are you looking at?" Beth asked.

"We're not sure," said Caroline. She crouched by the window, holding the binoculars up to her eyes. Then she giggled. *"Look* at them over there! They even have field glasses!"

Beth squeezed between Caroline and Eddie and looked where her sister was pointing. "They look like leprechauns," she said.

"They're boys," Eddie told her.

"How can you tell? They could be leprechauns, chimpanzees, creatures from the black lagoon . . ."

"But what are they most *likely* to be, Beth?" Eddie insisted. "Hand her the binoculars, Caroline."

Beth took the binoculars. "Boys," she answered.

"Right."

"Spying on us!" Beth said, starting to smile.

"Right again."

"What are we going to do?"

Eddie laughed. "Give them something to look at."

"But what?"

"We'll see," said Eddie.

Caroline smiled to herself. Whatever did girls do without sisters? She took the binoculars again and watched as the four boys across the river slowly made their way back down the trapdoor in the roof.

"Whatever we do, it's got to be good," said Eddie. "If they want a show, we'll give them something to talk about."

"Like what?" Beth insisted. "Dance naked around the yard?"

Eddie gave her a pained look and was quiet a moment, thinking. At last she said, "Somebody has to die, and Caroline's it."

"Eddie!"

"Oh, just pretend," Eddie told her.

Delicious goose bumps rose up on Caroline's arms. "I hope we don't go back to Ohio," she said aloud. "I hope we *never* go back. This is so much more exciting."

"Here's what we'll do," said Eddie. "We'll wait until we see them up there spying again. Then Beth and I will go down to the river carrying Caroline."

"In a sheet," said Beth. She went to her room for a notebook and pencil and returned, scribbling as she came. "We'll be carrying Caroline in a sheet and walking real slow, crying."

"Like one of those old silent movies! Oh, Beth, that's wonderful!" Caroline said.

"When we get to the river, we'll lay her down and cry some more," Eddie continued.

"And I'll have my arms folded over my chest. I'll look like this." Caroline closed her eyes and let her lips fall open just a fraction.

"We'll have to pray over her," Beth said. "We've got to take our time."

"Okay, but when it's over, we'll tip the sheet and slide you off into the river, Caroline. You're the best one to do it because you swim like a fish," Eddie told her.

"You'll have to hold your breath and sink deep down, then swim underwater for a ways," Beth cautioned. "Make sure you climb out far up-river where there are bushes to hide you."

"And the boys will think I'm dead!" Caroline said. "Eddie, this is the most wonderful idea you've ever had. But shouldn't I have flowers?"

Flowers, Beth wrote in her notebook.

"What if Mom sees us?" Caroline wondered.

"She won't," Eddie said. "She'll be so busy moving in, she won't know where we are half the time."

Caroline, Eddie, and Beth exchanged smiles and went downstairs to help. A wonderful script and an audience, ready and waiting, Caroline thought. What more could she possibly want?

▾ ▾ ▾

It was four days later that Beth rushed in with news. She had been reading a book back in the trees near the river when she saw the boys come over the swinging bridge and sneak along the bank on the Malloys' side.

"They were dragging a large plastic bag behind them, and dumped it on our bank, right at the edge of the water." Beth panted. "And do you know what was in it? Dead fish! Dead birds! Run-over squirrels and possums! The boys want us to think the river's polluted. I heard them talking!"

"Those creepy jerks!" cried Caroline.

"Those jerky creeps!" said Eddie. "This isn't a joke anymore. This is war!"

For two more days the girls spied on the boys. Whenever they passed a window, they looked. When they went to the old garage and climbed up in the loft, they kept one eye on the house across the river. And finally, on the third morning, when Mr. and Mrs. Malloy were debating whether Mother's plants or Father's trophies should go in the sunny room on the left side of the house, Caroline looked out and saw the four boys spying on them again from the widow's walk.

She rushed into the next room and told Eddie and Beth.

"Now!" whispered Eddie.

They got a bedsheet and took it to the kitchen. Taking off her shoes, Caroline lay down on it with her arms folded across her chest. Then Beth picked up the sheet at one end, Eddie picked up the other, and they moved slowly out the back door. Step by step, with heads bent, they walked somberly down the sloping hill toward the river.

They found a spot on the bank where they were sure the boys could still see them, and then—struggling hard to keep from laughing—gently laid the bedsheet down. Caroline hoped there were no dead fish or squirrels beneath her.

"Cry," whispered Beth.

"What?" murmured Caroline, barely moving her lips.

"Not you," said Beth. "Cry, Eddie."

Eddie wasn't so good at acting, but through half-closed eyes, Caroline saw her older sister put her hands to her face, her shoulders shaking. *Wonderful.*

Beth did it much better, of course. Beth even crawled over and kissed Caroline tenderly on the forehead. It was rather nice having her sisters weep over her. Even nicer when Beth picked a few wild-flowers and put them between her folded fingers. Both Beth and Eddie bowed their heads.

"Now I lay me down to sleep . . ." Eddie recited, and Beth joined in.

But then came the hard part. Caroline swallowed as she felt the sheet being lifted again. Her bottom bumped against the ground once or twice as she was carried down the bank.

Finally she felt her head begin to rise as the top

of the sheet was lifted, her feet begin to fall as the bottom of the sheet was lowered, and in what was the greatest performance of her life so far, Caroline Malloy, her body stiff as a board, eyes closed, arms still folded across her chest, slid all the way off the end of the sheet and into the chilly water.

Three

▼

Ghost

"Did you *see* that?"

Wally crouched on the balcony beside his brothers and stared.

At first it seemed as though the two older girls were dragging a sack of garbage, and then he saw that it was the girls' youngest sister. Dead! *Obviously* dead.

Wally looked wordlessly at Jake, his mouth hanging open. *They* had only thrown a few dead fish and squirrels and possums. The new folks were throwing people!

The boys couldn't hear across the river, of course, but they had studied the small girl lying there on the sheet and she hadn't moved a finger. Not a toe. The sisters were crying like crazy, and then, like a burial at sea, they'd dumped her in the river.

"I don't believe it!" said Jake hoarsely.

"In the *river*!" said Josh.

They sat with their eyes glued to the spot in the water where the body had disappeared. The body sank way down and did not come up again, and the two sisters were walking slowly back up the hill toward the house, arms around each other, heads down.

"They must have weighted her down with stones," breathed Jake.

Wally's throat was so dry, he could hardly get the words out. "What—what do you suppose she died of?" The answer, at the back of his mind, was too awful to say aloud.

"The—the water wasn't *that* polluted," murmured Josh.

"We only took over one bag of dead stuff," said Jake.

"Anyone with a grain of sense wouldn't drink that water or swim in a river with dead animals along the bank," Josh added.

But what if she didn't know? Wally wondered. What if she hadn't seen? What if she'd gone swimming one day farther down and the germs had been carried along in the current?

"M-maybe one of those dead squirrels had a disease," he suggested finally.

"Oh, man!" Josh rested his head in his hands. "Mom's going to have a fit."

"Well, we don't *know* that the dead fish and

stuff killed her, so we aren't going to tell," Jake declared hoarsely, and looked around at the others. "Okay? You got it? Not a word to *anybody*!"

"We can't even tell Mom the girl died?" asked Peter.

"No! Nothing! We'll wait to hear it from someone else."

Wally glanced over at Josh. He'd brought along his sketchbook because he liked to draw what houses and trees looked like from above. Josh drew things in his sketchbook that most guys never thought of drawing, but the page in front of him now was blank, and Wally was glad. He didn't want any evidence of what they had seen from the roof. If the girl had died because of what the boys had tossed on their bank, then Wally himself was a murderer because it had been his idea in the first place. He took a deep breath as he and his brothers climbed back inside.

▼ ▼ ▼

The boys were sitting soberly around the kitchen table, wondering who would find the body first, when their mother came in the back door.

"Good grief, is this how you're going to spend your last few days of vacation—just moping about?" She laid her car keys on the counter and opened the refrigerator. She had just thirty minutes to eat lunch and get back to her job at the hardware store.

"We've been busy—just taking a break," Josh told her.

"Busy doing what?" Mother asked.

Wally saw Jake give Peter a warning look. "Just messing around," Jake said.

As she passed out the sandwiches, Mother added, "I would have thought you'd be across the river by now, getting to know that new family."

"Fat chance," said Josh. "They're all girls."

"Really?" Mother looked around the table. "Somehow I had the idea there were boys."

"So did we," Jake told her.

"How many girls?" Mother asked.

"Two, now," Peter answered. "I mean three. *Three* girls!" He looked quickly at Jake. "*Three* girls, all right. I counted."

Mother studied him curiously.

"Well, at least they have children," she said, chewing thoughtfully. "It could have been worse. It could have been a family without any kids at all. I'd go over and make friends with them, if I were you."

"We will," said Jake, "when the Mississippi wears rubber pants to keep its bottom dry."

Josh laughed a little, and so did Mother, but Wally found it hard to smile at anything. Could you go to jail for planning a murder even if you didn't know anyone was going to die?

After Mother went back to work, the boys walked down to the river and followed it as far as the bridge. But they couldn't see a trace of a body— not bobbing about on the surface, not floating just beneath it, not caught in the roots of a tree or snagged on the branches that sometimes clogged the channel. The muddy water of the Buckman River moved lazily on, gracefully parting to make way for a rock here and there, then coming together again in its slow meander around the bend under the bridge.

When Father came home from work, Wally and his brothers were waiting for him on the steps. Mr. Hatford was a mailman in Buckman, and the boys knew that if anybody died anywhere at all in town, their father was one of the first to know.

"Hi, Dad," said Josh as Father came up the walk.

Mr. Hatford's shirt was damp, and he mopped his face with the small towel he carried over one shoulder in hot weather. The first thing he usually did when he got home was shower, but today he could scarcely make it into the house because the boys were blocking the steps.

"How y'doin'?" he said, maneuvering around them and going inside. The boys got up and followed him.

"Anything exciting happen today?" Jake inquired.

"I told Mrs. Blake I wouldn't deliver her mail unless she kept her dog in the house," Father said. "Almost got my pants torn off by that beast of hers. Other than that, no."

"Anybody die?" asked Peter. Wally reached over and pinched his arm, but it was too late.

"Not that I know of. Why? Did I miss something?"

"I guess we're getting bored," Jake said quickly. "Nothing exciting ever happens around here."

"Well, you could always go check out that new family," Father suggested. "Mr. Malloy is the new football coach at the college, I hear, and they've got three daughters about your ages."

"Did you meet them?" asked Josh.

"No, but I will before too long. Want me to say something for you?"

"No!" cried the four boys together.

Father smiled a little as he took off his shirt. "Okay, then. We'll just let things develop and see what happens."

What happens, Wally thought, is that someone's going to find the body, and someone is going to ask questions, and *someone*—namely Wally himself— was going to jail. All because of two words. Two words! *Dead fish.* He swallowed, but it didn't get rid of the rock in the pit of his stomach.

▼ ▼ ▼

On the last two days before school started, it seemed to Wally that he and his brothers were up on the widow's walk every waking moment, watching the new family through Mother's field glasses. He

14

knew their name now: Malloy. Sometimes Mrs. Malloy came out to empty the trash. Sometimes Mr. Malloy drove off in his car. Once in a while Jake or Josh would catch a glimpse of the two older sisters, but the younger one was nowhere in sight.

"Do you suppose she's *not* dead?" Wally asked hopefully. "Maybe they only thought she was dead, but the water revived her and she swam back to the bank."

"So why haven't we seen her around?" asked Jake. "Why do we see the two older sisters but we never see her?"

"She's sick, maybe?" suggested Peter.

"No, she's dead, all right," said Josh. He had drawn a picture of what the youngest Malloy girl would look like after being dead in the river for several days. Wally wished he hadn't drawn it, but Peter studied the picture with wide eyes.

If the Bensons were still here, Wally thought, they would have helped look for the body. *They* would have had some good ideas about where it could be. Then he remembered that if the Bensons were here, the Malloys would not be. What *would* he be doing if the Bensons were back?

Well, he decided, he and Bill Benson would probably have figured out by now what made the rows of little holes in the trunk of the pear tree. Sapsuckers, he had thought, but his friend had said bees. They had even been going to camp out all night and take turns watching, just to find out. Now they never would. Now there were girls to watch instead.

Wally spent most of his time lying in the grass behind the house, staring up at the sky. Peter lay down beside him.

"Do you see that spiderweb, Wally?" Peter asked, pointing to the thin strands of silver spun between a forsythia bush and a lilac. "Do you suppose the spider spins the cross ones first or the down ones?"

Wally often wondered that himself. "I think," he said, looking hard at the web, "that the spider sort of goes across and down at the same time—just drifts down hanging by a thread. Pretty clever, when you—"

"And if the thread breaks, splat!" said Peter delightedly, whapping one hand on the ground.

Wally sighed.

▾ ▾ ▾

Usually there was at least *some* excitement connected with going back to school in the fall. This year Mother had bought them all new T-shirts and jeans, and Wally and Peter had picked out new sneakers as well. But the boys hadn't put paper in their notebooks yet. They hadn't even sharpened their pencils. The big question among the boys was what they would say to the girls when the two remaining Malloy sisters walked across the bridge the next day on their way to school.

Mother didn't come home for lunch, so Jake

made beans and franks. "Why don't we watch from an upstairs window tomorrow, and when we see them start across the bridge, we'll time it so we get out to the road when they do. I just want to hear what they have to say about their sister," he said.

"What if they don't say anything?" Wally asked. "We don't even know their names. We can't just say, 'Hey, so-and-so, how's what's-her-name?'"

"We could say, 'How is the sister we saw rolled up in a bedsheet?'" Peter suggested. Josh shot him a disgusted glance, and Peter went back to lining the beans up in rows on his plate, then stabbing them three at a time with his fork.

The following morning Jake and Josh crouched at an upstairs window, watching the bridge. Peter, with his new lunch box, waited below.

Wally, however, was still dressing. As he put on his new sneakers, he realized that the treads were so deep, he could probably roll up a tiny piece of paper and stick it in a groove without it falling out. If he ever had to carry a secret somewhere, and there was any danger of being searched, he could always wear a new pair of sneakers and—

"They're coming!" Josh yelled.

Like a whirlwind the twins rushed downstairs, where Peter was waiting. With Wally bringing up the rear they all went outside.

The two older Malloy sisters, wearing jeans and long shirts down to their knees, were walking arm in arm across the swinging bridge, leaning on each other, heads together, like two girls who had more sadness than they could possibly bear, Wally thought.

As they came closer, the Hatford brothers pretended to be looking down the road, at the sky, anywhere, in fact, except at the Malloys.

"Ask!" Jake whispered to Josh.

"*You* ask!" said Josh. "You always try to make me do it."

"Wally, you do it," said Jake.

"Why me? What the heck am I supposed to say?"

The girls had reached the middle of the narrow bridge now and, still walking side by side, held on to the cable handrails as the bridge bounced slightly beneath their weight.

"If one of us doesn't ask, Peter will," Josh warned. "He'll say something dumb, like 'Have you buried anyone lately?'"

"I will not!" snapped Peter.

Wally didn't know what he'd say, but he knew that someone had to say something, so he stepped out in front of his brothers and started toward the bridge.

But suddenly there was nothing at all to say, because, as he stared, the two older Malloy girls stepped off the end of the bridge and the third Malloy sister popped out from behind them. She came right down the path to the very spot where Wally was standing. She had either never been dead at all or she was the first ghost in the history of Buckman, and here she was now, in front of his very eyes.

Four

▼

Conversation

"This," said Caroline to her sisters as the Hatford boys headed up the sidewalk, "was our greatest performance yet."

"What do you mean *yet*?" asked Beth, pulling a paperback from her bookbag to finish before school. *The Fog People*, it said on the cover. "I'm not going to spend all my time dropping you in the river and hiding you on the bridge."

"But they believed! They really, truly believed that I was dead and buried at sea! The look on their faces when I came out from behind you! If we could carry that off, we could do anything. We'd make a wonderful team!"

The four Hatford brothers were growing smaller and smaller in the distance. They hadn't said hello or 'Welcome to Buckman' or anything at all. They'd just gaped, their mouths wide open.

Eddie whirled her baseball cap around on one finger. "You *know* they'll try to get even."

"We *are* even! They dumped dead fish and squirrels on our side of the river, and we spooked them into thinking I was dead," said Caroline. She almost wished they *weren't* even, because she had so many wonderful scenes yet to play. There must be a hundred and fifty ways she and Beth and Eddie could fool the boys. Boys made such a wonderful audience. They'd believe anything.

Buckman Elementary was an old building of dark redbrick that didn't look anything like the new school they had left behind in Ohio.

"Quaint," said Beth, when she saw it.

"Dismal," Eddie proclaimed.

Caroline hadn't decided what to think about it until she passed the auditorium with its high stage and velvet curtain.

She stopped in her tracks and stared. Back in Ohio the only auditorium was the cafeteria. There the stage was a foot off the floor, with no curtain at all. But here there were fixed rows of seats for the audience, the kind you saw in movie theaters, and the curtain was maroon on one side, gold on the other. She knew positively when she saw it that somehow, sometime, on that very stage, she and Beth and Eddie would perform, and that she, Caroline Lenore Malloy, would have the leading role.

What she did *not* expect was that she would find

herself in the same classroom with one of the boys across the river. She didn't even know his name, but she recognized him from his sneakers that morning.

"Welcome to fourth grade," said a large woman at the front of the room—a woman as round and rosy as an apple, whose name was—incredible as it looked there on the blackboard—Miss Applebaum.

If Caroline weren't so precocious, she would have been entering the third grade, because she was only eight. But she had learned to read at four, subtract by five, and when she was six, she was in first grade only a month before she was transferred to second. If she was surprised to find herself in the same room with one of the boys across the river, however, the boy himself seemed even more astonished. His eyes grew as large as turnips when Caroline came through the door and his face turned petunia-pink.

"If you can remember just one thing, class, we'll get along famously," Miss Applebaum was saying. "When I talk, you listen. Now, the first thing we're going to do is seat you alphabetically."

I sure hope his last name isn't Mahony or something, Caroline thought, watching the boy.

Miss Applebaum was calling out names of students and pointing to seats, one after another, in the first row. She called out, "Wally Hatford," and pointed to the first seat in the second row, and the boy took it.

Wally Hatford, huh? Caroline said to herself.

Well, the Hatfords would soon find out they were no match for the Malloys. Miss Applebaum was filling up the rest of the second row, and when she called out, "Caroline Malloy," Caroline realized that the apple-shaped teacher was pointing to a desk directly behind Wally.

Caroline quietly took her seat, and hardly dared move. She was sure that the moment the teacher's back was turned, the boy would turn around and say something so awful, so embarrassing about Caroline and her sisters tricking him and his brothers that she would be forced to think of something awful and embarrassing to do to him next.

Wally did not turn around, however. He said nothing at all, and Caroline could not stand it. He kept his head pointing straight forward, hands on his desk, where he was holding a ruler between his thumbs, and as Miss Applebaum droned on and on, Caroline leaned forward and blew, ever so gently, at the fine hairs on the back of his neck.

This time she saw goose bumps break out on Wally's skin. Caroline smiled to herself. She leaned forward even farther until her mouth was just inches away from Wally's left ear, and then she said, "Wal-ly."

The boy did not move, but his ear—*both* ears—turned bright red.

"Wal-ly," Caroline whispered again, just behind him. "There is a gigantic black spider with eight hairy legs dropping down from the ceiling about five inches above your head."

"Where?" Wally said, throwing back his head, and crashed right into Caroline's nose.

"Ow!" she yelped, covering her face.

"Caroline Malloy and Wally Hatford!" said Miss Applebaum. "I don't believe either of you is paying the slightest attention. What's wrong?"

"There was a big spider coming down from the ceiling over my head," said Wally. "She told me."

He seemed to be trying hard not to smile, but Caroline could hardly think because her nose ached so.

Miss Applebaum came down the aisle and stood beside her. "Let's see this gigantic spider," she said dryly. "A spider like that we should study in science. Where is it?"

"Gone, I guess," Caroline said, still holding her nose. It was bleeding a little. She hoped it wasn't broken. Actresses with broken noses never got the good parts.

"Since Caroline and Wally have cost us some class time, I think it would be fair for them to stay after school and make it up," said Miss Applebaum. "If you see any more big hairy spiders, Caroline, you may collect them in a paste jar. And if you hear any other girls telling you about spiders descending over your head, Wally, I suggest you pay no attention whatever. Do you want to see the nurse, Caroline?"

"No." Caroline answered, snuffling, and spent the rest of class with a tissue wadded beneath her nose.

She didn't see her sisters all morning. When the fourth grade was doing arithmetic, the fifth and sixth grades were having recess. When the fourth grade was having recess, the fifth and sixth grades were having lunch.

It was halfway through the afternoon when Caroline happened to pass Eddie's class in the hall on the way to the library. She grabbed her sister's arm and said, "Eddie, is my nose broken?"

"What?"

"Is it crooked?"

"No. What happened?"

"Wally Hatford."

"What?" cried Eddie, but by this time her classmates were well down the hall, and she had to run to catch up.

What bothered Caroline most about her predicament was that she wouldn't be able to walk home with Beth and Eddie, and would have to wait to tell them about Wally Hatford banging her nose.

At three o'clock everyone left except Caroline and Wally.

"What is so wrong about not listening when I'm talking," Miss Applebaum told them, "is that you disturb other students as well."

Caroline stared down at her desktop. She wondered how old it was. There were all kinds of things scratched in the wood—initials and numbers and little cartoon faces.

"And because listening is the most important thing in my class, and talking out of turn is so distracting," Miss Applebaum continued, "I want to make sure it doesn't happen again. Come up here, both of you."

Caroline got woodenly to her feet. Miss Applebaum wasn't going to paddle them, was she? She didn't think she could stand the humiliation. Wasn't that against the law? Or could teachers do things like that in West Virginia?

She followed Wally up front where Miss Applebaum was placing two chairs, face to face, about three feet apart.

"I want you to sit here," she told them, "and I want you to talk to each other for ten minutes. Perhaps at the end of that time you will have said everything there is to say, and there will be no more disturbances in class."

No! Caroline thought. She would rather be paddled! One minute would be bad enough, five minutes would be cruel and unusual punishment, and ten was torture!

She lowered herself sideways into one of the chairs. What was she supposed to say to a boy who, up until that morning, had thought she was dead?

Miss Applebaum stood with arms folded. "Well? I'm waiting."

Caroline crossed her ankles. "You started it," she said to Wally.

"What did *I* do?" he mumbled, sitting sideways himself.

"Dumping all that dead stuff on our side of the river."

"So *you* pretended to die."

"Is this a normal conversation?" asked Miss Applebaum as she picked up a box of supplies and headed for the closet at the back of the room.

"No," said Caroline, but she was talking to Wally, not her teacher. "This is not a normal conversation because you and your brothers aren't normal human beings. Normal people don't go dumping dead fish and birds around the neighborhood."

"It wasn't my idea," said Wally. "Well, actually it *was* my idea—dead fish, I mean—but it was Jake and Josh who—"

"So *none* of you are normal."

"*We're* not normal?" said Wally, his voice rising. "What do you call people who go burying each other in the river?"

"It was a great performance, and you know it."

"It was dumb."

"You believed I was dead."

"I believe you're crazy."

"We'll see about that."

"Whatever you two are arguing about, you'd better get it out of your systems now, because when you come to school tomorrow, I expect you to pay attention," Miss Applebaum called, sticking her head out of the supply closet.

"You and your dumb brothers," Caroline muttered because she couldn't think of anything else to say.

"You and your stupid sisters," said Wally.

"We're smarter than the four of you put together," Caroline told him.

"We'll see," said Wally.

"If you'd just left us alone instead of dumping that dead stuff, things would be okay," said Caroline.

"If you'd go back where you came from, there wouldn't be any more trouble," Wally replied.

"Oh, yeah? If you went back to where *you* came from, you'd be in a cave!"

"That does it," said Wally, hotly. "The war is on."

"Okay," called Miss Applebaum, coming back to the front of the room for another box. "If you two have settled things, you may leave now." She looked from Caroline to Wally. "Unless, of course, you are not agreed."

"We agree," said Caroline emphatically. *The war is definitely on.*

She could hardly wait to get home and tell her sisters.

What she discovered when she got outside was that she wasn't the only member of her family who had been kept after school. Eddie had stumbled over Jake's foot in the cafeteria and, sure that he'd tripped her on purpose, brought her tray down on his head. Beth, of course, had waited for Eddie, so there they were again, the three of them coming home late on the very first day.

Mother was dusting shelves in the hallway. "Whatever happened to your nose?" she asked, looking at Caroline.

"She bumped into something that needs a little fixing," said Beth.

"Needs a lot of straightening out," put in Eddie.

"Well, how was school?" Mother asked.

"Urk," said Eddie.

"Ugh," said Beth.

"It has possibilities," said Caroline.

Five

▼

Peace Offering

Peter, Josh, and Jake were waiting in the bushes when Wally came around the bend.

"What happened?" asked Jake. "The Malloys just stomped by, mad as anything."

Wally was miserable. "I just declared war," he said, and told them what had happened.

"Hoo boy!" Josh whistled.

"Wow!" said Peter.

For the rest of the way home Jake and Josh talked about what they would do if the Malloys tried to get even with Wally for bumping Caroline's nose. They were in the same class with Eddie.

"That Eddie would try anything," said Jake. "If she'd dump her tray on me in front of teachers and everybody, you can imagine what she'd do when no one was looking."

"Did you watch her pitch at recess? Whomp!

The ball comes at you before you can look at it cross-eyed," Josh went on.

"Who's the other sister?" Peter asked, walking fast to keep up.

"Beth," Josh told him. "She's weird. Sits on the steps at recess and reads a book."

"A Whomper, a Weirdo, and a Crazie," said Jake, and sighed. "I wonder how the Benson guys are doing down in Georgia. I'll bet they miss us like anything."

When they reached the house, Wally took a box of crackers up to his room and sat on the floor to eat them, his back against his bed. He still couldn't believe that he was the one who had officially declared war on the Malloys. How had it happened? Only a week before he was lying on his back in the grass, and now here he was: Number One on their Most-Wanted list. He was on bad terms already with his teacher, had almost broken Caroline's nose, and had made everything worse by calling her sisters stupid.

Well, they *were* stupid. And deep down, seven layers beneath his skin, Wally knew he was glad that he had thrust his head back and bumped Caroline. He'd just wanted her to stop bugging him, that's all. But her nose sure looked peculiar by the end of the day—a lot redder and fatter than it had looked that morning.

Then he had another thought: What if it really was broken, she had to have an operation, and he had to pay for it? His hands began to sweat, and he swallowed the piece of cracker in his mouth without chewing. Was there such a thing as just a sprained nose? A bruised nose? A slightly but not completely fractured nose? A bent nose, maybe?

Peter came into Wally's room and sat down beside him on the rug.

"What are we going to do next?" he asked excitedly, helping himself to a cracker. He rested one hand on Wally's leg, looking up at his older brother.

What Wally wanted to do, in fact, was sit on this rug for the rest of his natural life and never have to face the Malloys again.

"You're the general," said Peter.

"Huh?"

"That's what Josh said. He said you're the one who declared the war, so you've got to call the shots. That's what he said, all right."

Wally gave a low moan.

"What I think we should do," said Peter, "is dig a large hole and cover it with leaves and sticks, and when Caroline and her sisters walk across it, they'll fall in and we'll keep them trapped forever."

"Go out and play, Peter," Wally told him.

▼ ▼ ▼

The boys were strangely quiet when their father came home from his mail route about four. Jake was planning strategies in a notebook, Josh was drawing a picture of Eddie dropping her tray on Jake, just for the record, and Peter was building a pit out of toothpicks, then running a Matchbox car over it and watching the car tumble in. Wally was looking out the window, wondering how far away he could get if he climbed on the first Greyhound through town.

Mr. Hatford took off his cap and went out to the kitchen for a Mountain Dew. Then he leaned against the doorway and looked at the boys. "You'll be interested to know that the Malloy girls are Eddie, Beth, and Caroline."

"*Tell* me about it," Jake mumbled.

"The way their mother described them, they sound like three live wires to me."

"Crossed wires is more like it," said Josh.

"Short circuits," said Wally.

"A Whomper, a Weirdo, and a Crazie," Peter repeated.

Mr. Hatford frowned. "You boys can either make yourselves miserable by wishing the Bensons were back, which they're not, or you can enjoy a great September day, which it is. And I, for one, aim to enjoy the day." He took his soft drink out onto the side porch along with the paper.

Jake looked at Josh. "I'll bet they'll spread it all over town how they tricked us. Everyone will be laughing."

"You know what we could do, don't you?" said Josh. "Totally ignore them. Freeze them out. Not even give them the time of day."

▲▽▲▽▲▽▲▽▲▽▲▽

"If we see them coming, we could just turn and walk the other way," said Peter.

"We can't," said Jake. "Wally declared war."

"Oh, yeah. Right," said Josh.

Hoo boy! thought Wally.

▼ ▼ ▼

The hardware store was open till nine most evenings, and this was Mrs. Hatford's night to work. When she popped in about six to make dinner, she said, "Boys, I've got a job for you. I baked a cake this morning before work, frosted it at noon, and I want you to take it over to the Malloys right now so they can have some with their supper."

Wally stared at his mother as though she had just grown another head.

"Well, don't look so astonished," she said, coming out of the kitchen with a large square box. "It's the traditional way to greet a new family in the neighborhood, you know. The Bensons did it for us the first week we moved in, and I'll never forget how good that cake tasted after unpacking all day."

"But—" Wally began.

"Just hand it to whoever answers the door, tell them it's from the Hatfords, and say, 'Welcome to Buckman.' That's all you have to say. Then come right home because dinner's almost ready."

"Could we—could we just leave it on their porch?" Wally asked.

"Wallace Hatford, you certainly may not!" his mother scolded. "A dog could get into it, there might be a rain . . . all sorts of things could happen. What's the matter with saying a few cordial words to a new family? Hurry up, now. Who's going to take it over?"

Wally looked at Jake, who was looking at Josh, and then they all turned toward Peter.

"Peter is not going over there alone. This is a three-layer chocolate chiffon with whipped cream frosting, and I worked on it a total of two hours and set it on the plate I got from Aunt Ida at Christmas. I want to make sure it gets there in one piece. You can *all* go. Hold this box steady, now," she instructed, thrusting it into Wally's hands. "If the cake slides around, the icing will come off on the sides of the box. Tell them there's no hurry about returning the plate."

Wally and his brothers moved down the front steps as though they were headed for a funeral and Wally carried the remains of the deceased in the box. *This can't be happening*, he said to himself, but it was. After half breaking Caroline's nose, this would look as though he were saying he was sorry. He was *not* sorry, and now he was mad as anything.

"If Caroline comes to the door, Wally, let her have it," said Jake. "Swoosh! Right in the schnozz. It'll be worth the whipping we get when we go home."

"Uh-uh," said Josh. "Dad'll march us back over there and make us apologize, and that would be worse."

"*You* take it," Wally said, holding the box out toward Jake. "Eddie dropped her tray on you in the cafeteria, and you could drop this on her. We'd just say we were getting even."

"No way. I'd still have to apologize, and I'm not about to apologize to Eddie Malloy if someone burned my feet with hot irons."

"Wow!" said Peter, impressed.

They walked down the sidewalk, crossed the road, and started along the bank toward the swinging footbridge.

"I know what we can do," Wally said at last. "We could creep over to their front porch, set the cake in front of the door, then ring the bell and run. That way we wouldn't have to say anything at all."

"*If* we can get over there without their seeing us," said Josh.

"Here's what we'll do," Jake told them. "Once we get across the bridge, we'll stay off Island Avenue and keep to the bushes along the river. When we get opposite their house, we'll put the cake on the porch when no one's watching."

"This isn't any fun," grumbled Peter. "I thought this was a war."

"Just a temporary cease-fire," Jake assured him.

The boys had just stepped onto the swinging bridge and started across when Wally's heart almost stopped beating, for coming down the hill on the other side were the three Malloy sisters, and a moment later they, too, were on the bridge.

For a moment everybody stopped, the Hatfords at one end, the Malloys at the other.

"Now what?" whispered Wally.

"They're trying to block us," said Jake. "Just keep going. If they want a fight, they'll get it."

The boys started forward again. The girls moved forward too.

The swinging bridge bounced and jiggled as the two groups came toward each other. Wally held on to the cable with one hand, the cake with the other. He'd never fought a girl in his life. None of his brothers had, either, and he knew that for all of Jake's talk, they wouldn't begin now. This was a different kind of battle—a war of the wits.

But what if the girls didn't see it that way? What if the Malloys got out in the middle of the bridge and trashed them? Could they fight back then?

The Hatford brothers had fallen into single file as they approached the middle of the bridge. You always did that when you met someone coming toward you; always said hello and moved over to make room. The Malloy girls, however, came in a row.

"The first one who tries anything gets the cake right in the puss," Jake whispered in Wally's ear.

The next thing Wally knew, he was face to face with Caroline Malloy—face to nose, anyway, for her swollen nose seemed to take up half her face. It had also turned black and blue. He realized suddenly that if he just gave the girls the cake, he wouldn't have to walk all the way over to their house. He wouldn't have to ring the doorbell and say nice things to the parents. He wouldn't have to fight the girls to get on across either.

"Here," he said, holding the box out in front of him. "It's a cake."

Caroline stared at him, then at her sisters.

"It's a *cake*!" Wally said again. "It's for you."

"Yeah?" said Eddie.

"I'll just bet!" said Beth. "What dead animal did you dream up this time?"

Suddenly Caroline grabbed the box out of Wally's hands and, in one swift toss, flung it over the side of the bridge.

Wally and his brothers stared in astonishment as Mother's three-layer chocolate chiffon spilled out into the water, the two top layers heading in different directions. The box—with the bottom layer still in it—bobbed up and down in the current, and the whipped cream frosting, like foam, floated downstream.

Six

▼

The River on Caroline

Caroline and her sisters stood with their hands over their mouths, eyes like fried eggs.

"Oh, Lordy!" gasped Caroline. "It really *was* a cake!"

The box below was sailing away.

"Enjoy!" said Wally, grinning. "Don't forget to return the plate."

With that the four Hatford brothers turned around and went back toward their side of the river, though the youngest lingered just long enough for one last look in the water. "Wow!" he said.

"What are we going to *do?*" Caroline cried to her sisters.

"Don't ask *me!*" said Beth. "You're the one who threw it in."

"But you didn't believe it was a cake, either, Beth. You know you didn't!"

"We're in this together," Eddie agreed. *"I* probably would have taken the box and dumped it over their heads."

"I suppose we could always say we ate it," Caroline mused, watching the whipped cream frosting leave a long trail in its wake. And then she cried suddenly, "The plate! We've got to return the plate!"

The box seemed to be floating toward the Malloys' side of the river. The girls ran back across the bridge and down the bank to the water's edge.

"There it is!" Eddie shouted. She looked at Caroline. "Go for it."

"It's not fair!" Caroline cried. "We're in this together, you said."

"Okay, we *all* go in," decided Eddie, and the girls took off their shoes and socks, and rolled up their jeans.

The water did not seem as warm as it had been a week ago when Caroline slid off the sheet and disappeared into the muddy brown of the Buckman River. Now it was almost six in the evening, August had become September, and that little change made a difference.

The riverbed was rocky in places, and where it was bare, thick mud oozed up between Caroline's toes. Now and then something tickled her ankles as she waded out toward the center, and she did not even like to think what it might be.

The box had stopped at a pile of brush in the river, but one corner appeared to be sinking.

"Hurry, Caroline!" Beth yelled, plodding along behind.

Caroline took a deep breath and waded in up to her waist. The more water-logged her jeans became, the heavier they felt, and the harder it was to walk.

"Hurry!" Beth screeched again.

Caroline took a giant step forward this time, but her foot slipped on the slimy bottom. The last thing she saw before the water washed over her was the white box rising up over the debris with the current, and sailing on downstream.

Glub, glub, glub. Water filled her ears, her nose —clouded her eyes. Gasping, she reared up, all her clothes heavy now. Before she could see anything, however, she could hear shrieks of laughter from the opposite bank, and knew that the Hatford boys had been watching.

"We'll get *them*!" Eddie called. "Don't pay any attention, Caroline. Just get the plate."

But the box was moving faster than the girls could keep up, and—what's more—seemed to be sinking slowly at the same time. More hoots from the boys. Caroline began to swim.

Caroline Lenore, she told herself, *you are an actress, and actresses don't pay any attention to distractions. Make this your greatest performance yet.*

And so, as she swam toward the center of the Buckman River where she had last seen the box, she pretended that she was a young mother swimming, swimming, desperately swimming, to rescue her small child before he disappeared forever beneath the waves.

Caroline tried to concentrate on her face. She would have a look of agonized terror, she decided, opening her eyes wide, teeth frozen behind half-parted lips, little gasps coming from her throat. She could see the Hatford boys back on the far bank, watching.

The camera would move in for a close-up of her face, and just then she would close her eyes, and . . . plunge. Caroline went tail up like a duck, diving beneath the surface, her arms outstretched, feeling for a box or a china plate. Once she thought she touched it, but it was only the slimy moss of a rock.

"There it goes!" shouted Beth, pointing farther downstream as Caroline surfaced. "Oh, m'gosh, it's headed for the rocks!"

Her baby! Her poor baby! The cameras still rolling in her head, Caroline plunged forward again, arms battling the water as she stroked. Faster, faster . . . her only child! In another minute he would be dashed against the rocks.

Out of the corner of her eye she could see the Hatford boys going home. They weren't even going to stay till the end! No matter. A good actress played her part whether or not the entire theater was empty. On she swam.

The box came apart just before the largest rock in the river came into view. She could see the plate spilling out, sinking, and she lunged. She had it!

She'd found him! She'd rescued her little baby, her heart's delight!

Holding the plate against her chest, Caroline crawled up on the rock and swooned.

"For corn's sake, Caroline, cut the comedy!" Eddie yelled, swimming toward her. She and Beth reached the rock and climbed up beside Caroline, who collapsed dramatically against them, going limp in their arms.

"Caroline, knock it off!" Eddie said sternly. "Is the plate okay?"

The mood was broken; the show was over. Caroline blinked, her hair streaming water into her eyes, and examined the plate. It still had a sticker on the bottom, as though it were new, and there was a dainty scalloped design around the edge—the kind of plate her mother used for cookies at Christmas, or served little sandwiches on when she entertained the faculty wives. Miraculously it was not broken, but there was a fine hairline crack in the surface. "It's okay, I guess," she told Eddie.

Eddie and Beth slipped into the water again, and Caroline reluctantly followed, swimming back to the bank behind her sisters.

"What are we going to tell Mom?" Beth asked as they put on their socks and sneakers. "What will we say about the cake?"

"Never mind the cake, what will we tell her about *us*?" said Eddie. "Look at us! Soaked to the skin!"

Dinner at the Malloys was almost never before seven, because Coach Malloy had football practice until six-thirty every evening in the fall. The girls had just time enough to rush upstairs to shower and change before they saw his car making its way down Island Avenue, to park at last in the clearing between the house and garage.

He slid into his chair at the table. "You girls look as though you'd been swimming" was the first thing out of his mouth.

"In *that* river?" asked Mother, placing a roast before them.

"I just took a shower," said Beth, which was the honest truth.

"Me too," said Eddie.

"Well, that's where I'm headed after dinner," their father said. "I don't know if I've got a team or not, Jean, they all seem pretty green to me. But I'll tell you one thing, I'm going to make them one by the first of October."

"Of course you will," said Mrs. Malloy. "You know, I sort of like living in a small town like this."

"*I* think it stinks," said Eddie, reaching for the pepper.

Her mother looked up. "Why, Edith Ann?"

"It's a town full of dumb boys, is what it is, and I pitched better than any boy at recess today, but I *still* have to try out for the baseball team."

▲▼▲▼▲▼▲▼▲▼▲▼▲▼

"It's only fair," said her father. "Have you met any of the neighbors?"

"I have," said Mrs. Malloy. "The people next door are friendly. And I met our mailman for the first time, a Mr. Hatford. He says he lives across the river, and his wife works at Grady's Hardware. By and by, I imagine, we'll meet them all."

Caroline looked at Beth and Eddie and said nothing. But after dinner, when Mother went upstairs to write some letters and the girls were on kitchen duty, she said, "You know what we have to do, don't you? Return the plate."

"You know what will happen if the boys answer the door; they'll take the plate, break it, and tell their mother we did it," Beth said.

"Then we've got to make sure the mother's there when we ring the doorbell. In fact, we'll ask to talk to her," said Caroline.

Eddie went to the telephone in the hall and looked up the number for Grady's Hardware, then dialed. "What time do you close?" she asked.

"Nine o'clock," a man told her.

Eddie hung up and looked at the others. "We leave here at nine-fifteen, and we'd better figure out exactly what we're going to say."

"Right!" said Caroline. "Beth, you write the script, and we'll practice it a couple times first."

▼ ▼ ▼

At a quarter past nine the girls crossed the bridge in the moonlight, the plate securely in Eddie's hands. It was a beautiful night, almost too lovely to be angry at anyone, Caroline thought. Beth must have felt the same way because, halfway over, she said, "Why do you suppose the Hatford boys hate us so much?"

"I don't think they *hate* us," Caroline mused. "I'll bet they're just mad that the Bensons moved out and we moved in. The Bensons had all boys, you know."

"Well, too bad!" Eddie snapped. "I didn't ask to come here any more than they wanted me to."

"I suppose we *could* just ring the doorbell and say, 'Look, let's bury the hatchet and be friends,'" Beth suggested.

The girls looked at each other and smiled a little.

"Naw," said Caroline. "This is a lot more fun."

The porch light was still on when the Malloy girls went up the steps to the Hatfords' large porch, which wrapped around three sides of the house. Through the curtains they could see Mr. Hatford stretched out on the couch, watching TV, and a boy somewhere in the background, who seemed to be doing his homework at the dining-room table.

Caroline pressed the button. The doorbell chimed. Footsteps. The door opened. And there was Wally Hatford, his eyes wide.

"Who is it, Wally?" came a woman's voice in the background.

"It—it's . . ."

▲▼▲▼▲▼▲▼▲▼▲▼▲▼

"Who?"

A woman appeared and Wally disappeared—disappeared as though the floor had opened and swallowed him up.

"Hello, Mrs. Hatford," Caroline said sweetly. "We came to return your cake plate."

"My goodness, so soon? There was no hurry."

"It was wonderful," said Beth. "Chocolate is my favorite. Chocolate cake with whipped cream frosting."

"Well, it was an old recipe, but it always works well for me. Chocolate chiffon, it was, to be exact." Mrs. Hatford looked pleased.

"Right. Chocolate chiffon," said Eddie. "Thanks a lot."

"We want our neighbors to feel welcome," Mrs. Hatford told her. "If there is anything at all we can do to help you get settled, we'd be glad to. The boys, also."

An actress, Caroline knew, had to be ready to ad-lib when the occasion arose, and that occasion was now.

"Oh, I know there would be lots of things Dad could use boys for, seeing as how he has only girls," Caroline said.

"Well, you just let us know—any chores at all," said Mrs. Hatford. "Call us anytime, and I'll send them right over."

Seven

▼

Free-for-all

Wally stood motionless in the hallway as his mother closed the door.

"Well, they certainly must have enjoyed that cake, to eat it all in one meal," she said. She turned the plate over in her hands, then frowned. "My goodness, it's cracked! You'd think they would have taken better care of it, wouldn't you?"

Wally started to tell her what had happened to the plate, but stopped. If he said any more, he'd have to explain why the girls had thrown it in the river. And if he told why, he'd have to tell about the dead fish and the way he'd banged Caroline's nose in class.

"They probably fed it to a dog," he said lamely.

Mother wheeled about. "Wallace, I don't know what's got into you lately. *All* you boys have been on edge. Maybe you don't have enough to do. Need a few extra chores around here."

Hoo boy! thought Wally as he went upstairs.

This evening sure hadn't turned out the way he'd wanted. He and his brothers had had a laughing fit watching Caroline out there in the river, trying to find that plate. He never thought she would, and the boys would have waited around if they hadn't remembered that dinner was on the table.

Wally lay on his stomach on his bed and stared down at the braided rug. Ordinarily he would have tried to figure out just how the little loops of orange got hooked onto the loops of green—where it all began, and which piece you'd have to pull first if you wanted the whole thing to come unraveled, but now he was too mad at the Malloys to give it much thought.

He'd like to pull a loop on the Malloy sisters, that's what, and watch them come apart for once. He'd like to see them pack their bags and take off out of town at seventy miles an hour.

It just wasn't like it was when the Bensons lived in Buckman. Back then they always signed each other's notebooks on the first day of school—the Hatfords and the Bensons. They'd give each other new nicknames for the year, and once they'd all taken the names of football players. That was the year Wally had been Joe Montana. Things were sure different now. Caroline and her black-and-blue nose! Eddie and that dumb cap! Beth and those stupid books she read.

She'd left one on the steps a few minutes at recess, Josh had reported, and he'd seen the cover: *Fang, King of the Vampires*. What kind of a girl would read a book like that? Weirdo was right.

▼ ▼ ▼

When the Hatford boys were ready for school the next day, they watched until the Malloys were across the bridge and well up the sidewalk before they set out themselves.

"You see what's happening, don't you?" Jake grumbled. "They're running our lives! They've only been here a week, and already we can't even leave for school when we want; we make sure they've got there first."

"And Mom thinks they're nice! They're poison!" said Josh.

Wally did not turn around in his seat once to look at Caroline, and she didn't bother him—no blowing on the back of his neck or whispering in his ear. At lunchtime he sat as far away from her table as he could get, and when he left at the end of the day, Miss Applebaum said, "Thank you, Wally, for being a good listener." He could have puked.

Jake and Josh and Peter were waiting for him when he came out. Josh had a smile on his face.

"What have *you* got to grin about?" Wally asked.

"At recess this afternoon," Josh told him, "I went inside for a drink of water, and when I came out again, there's Beth, on the bottom step, reading her stupid book."

"Fang, King of the Vampires?" Wally asked.

Josh nodded and grinned even wider. "I had my jacket tied around my shoulders, and when I spread out my arms, I looked like a giant bat. All I did was come slowly down the steps behind her, and she screamed her head off. I didn't even touch her."

Jake and Wally and Peter all laughed.

"You get caught?" asked Wally.

"No, but boy, was she mad! She said this was exactly the kind of thing that gives her nightmares, and I said, well, why did she read books like that if they gave her nightmares? Stupid thing!"

"Ha!" said Jake.

Home again, Wally had just poured himself a glass of Hi-C, and the boys were making peanut-butter-and-cracker sandwiches, when the phone rang. Wally answered.

"Listen," came his mother's voice, and she was beginning to sound like Miss Applebaum. "Your father was talking with Mrs. Malloy this morning on his route, and she wondered who she could hire to wash their windows. Dad told her you boys have more time on your hands than is good for you, and that you'd come over after school and help. Now, I don't want you to expect payment."

Wally yelped.

"Wally?" said his mother.

"It's not fair!" he shouted. "They've got three girls who could wash windows. Eddie can climb up a ladder as well as any of us, and she's even taller than Josh. Besides, I've got plenty of things to do!"

"Name one," said his mother.

Wally stood speechless. He didn't have any homework to do; he didn't play on any team. He didn't even need a haircut. He did, of course, still want to see how long it took a waffle box to go around the river, but . . .

"Wallace Hatford, you and your brothers have yourselves a snack and get on over to the Malloys'. With the four of you working, you could have their windows done in no time, and it's the least we can do for new neighbors. Why, when we moved in, the Bensons came over and helped us wallpaper the dining room. I'll never forget it. And I don't want to hear any arguments."

The receiver clicked, and Wally stood staring at the phone in his hand. He didn't have to tell the others; they'd already heard.

"We've got to wash their windows, right?" said Josh.

"Right," said Wally. "I'll bet Caroline put her mother up to this! Went right home and told her how much we wanted to help! And Dad probably said we'd do it for nothing."

"I'll wash their windows, all right," muttered Jake. "I'll put out their lights, curl their hair, and knock them into the middle of next week."

"Gosh!" said Peter.

"They're getting too cocky!" Jake went on.

"Those girls think they can get away with anything. They need a good scare, that's what. Then maybe they'll leave us alone."

"But how?" asked Peter.

Everyone turned to Wally.

"I'll think of something," Wally told them.

▼ ▼ ▼

By the time they finished their snack and headed off toward the Malloys', the boys had given up any idea of trying to scare the entire family. But they *were* convinced that they could scare Beth half out of her mind, and the thought of it, the vision of it, the sweet taste of victory in their mouths, made the idea of washing all the Malloys' windows worth it, every window.

It would have been better, of course, if Caroline, Beth, and Eddie were not smirking at them as they came across the lawn. Were not, in fact, sitting on a blanket out on the grass, sunning themselves, with cookies and soft drinks beside them, ready to enjoy the show.

"I'm so glad to meet you," said Mrs. Malloy, coming down the steps. "Your dad said you were the best window washers around, and I think it's wonderful the way you offered to help."

Wally didn't know whether he imagined it or whether he really did hear a snicker from Caroline.

"You do know each other, don't you?" Mrs. Malloy went on, motioning to the girls on the lawn.

"Eddie, Beth, and Caroline, this is . . ." She paused, waiting for the boys to say their own names.

"Josh," said Jake.

"Jake," said Josh.

"Peter," said Wally.

"Wally," said Peter.

Wally could hardly keep from grinning. Caroline looked at him and then at her mother, but she didn't say anything and Wally knew why. If the girls squealed, the boys would tell about the cake. Even-Steven.

Mrs. Malloy turned toward the house. "We have these to do," she said, "as well as the storm windows there in the garage. We might as well do them all."

Wally stared in dismay. There were twenty windows at least on the house, which meant twenty storm windows more stored in the garage. This time he heard a *definite* snicker from the girls on the grass.

"The girls will help, of course," said their mother, and Caroline's smile disappeared in an instant. So did Beth's and Eddie's. "What you boys can do is get the ladder from the garage and soap each window. Eddie can turn the hose on them from below to rinse them, and you can dry them after that. Beth and Caroline will change the water whenever you need it, and get clean rags. With all seven of you working together, I doubt it should

take more than a couple of hours. I'll have doughnuts and cider for you when you're done."

When Mrs. Malloy went inside for the bucket
and rags, Jake looked over at Eddie: "Nice going."
He smirked.

Eddie tossed her head and looked away.

▼ ▼ ▼

The old garage leaned a little to one side, but
Wally didn't mind. It was his favorite place on the
Bensons' property, and he and his brothers and the
Benson boys used to play in there for hours. For a
time they'd turned it into a club house, and other
times it had become a hideout. It was dark and
musty, with loose boards that creaked in the wind.

He and Jake carried the ladder from the garage
and put it up to the first window of the house where
Mrs. Malloy was pointing. Eddie glumly got out the
hose, and after Mrs. Malloy supervised the cleaning
of the first window, she went back inside.

"Which window is yours, Eddie?" Josh called
down. "I'll be sure to leave lots of smudges on it."

"Har, har," said Eddie.

The reason the work went so quickly was because no one spoke much after that. Wally had read
once about an order of monks who went about their
work in silence and never spoke except for one hour
on Friday evenings. This must be what it was like to
be a monk, he decided as he carried the last of the
storm windows out of the garage, except that there
wouldn't be any girl monks around.

Josh did the climbing of the ladder, Beth kept him supplied with clean water and rags, Jake and Wally carried storm windows in and out of the garage, Eddie hosed them off, and Caroline and Peter wiped the storm windows clean. In and out, up and down, back and forth. . . .

Mrs. Malloy had been right about one thing—the work *did* go faster with so many of them helping. Once, as he passed Caroline, she looked so cheerful, he was about to tell *her* about the monks who never talked except for an hour on Friday evenings, but then he remembered she was the enemy, so he told Jake instead.

"If there were girl monks, you know what they'd be called?" he asked, grinning. "Monk-ees."

Jake laughed out loud.

It was then that it happened, but no one knew quite how. It might have been Jake's laugh that made Eddie turn, hose in hand, but as she did, the water made a loop in the air and caught Josh, up on the ladder. His bucket came crashing to the ground with a splash, two inches away from Beth, soaking her to the skin with brown, dirty water.

While Wally stared, Beth pushed a sponge in Jake's face, Peter rushed to help his brother, Caroline went to help her sisters, and Wally simply tried to get the hose out of Eddie's hand. It was spewing water in every direction. The next great battle of the war had begun.

66

"Hey, what's this?" cried Mrs. Malloy, coming out of the house. "Girls! Stop it!"

Wally, who had the hose now, was holding it upright like a pitchfork, and realized that water was cascading down onto Mrs. Malloy's flower bed. As he jerked it away, he sent a stream of water across the porch, catching the girls' mother right in the face.

Wally gasped.

Spluttering, Mrs. Malloy rushed down the steps and turned off the faucet, then stood there shaking water from her clothes.

"Now, what's this all about?" she demanded.

"They started it, Mom," said Caroline, wringing out the tail of her shirt.

"We did not!" said Jake hotly. "Eddie turned the hose on Josh."

"He dropped his bucket on purpose!" cried Beth.

"I did not!" said Josh.

Mrs. Malloy looked around curiously. "You kids hardly know each other! How did you get to be enemies so soon?"

Wally looked at Caroline. *I dare you*, his eyes told her. No one spoke for a moment.

"Just fooling around, Mom," said Caroline.

"Yeah, just goofing off," Eddie murmured.

"Nobody's hurt," added Beth.

"Well, let's finish up that last window, then, and have some refreshment," Mrs. Malloy said.

For a moment they all looked as though they were going to laugh, Wally thought. They *did* look funny, with their heads dripping water, their clothes soaking wet. And when Mrs. Malloy brought out the doughnuts and cider, and they sat on the steps to eat, he thought, for maybe one fifth of a second, that the war might be over.

That was before Mrs. Malloy went back inside, however. That was before the boys started home. Because they had not gone ten feet from the house when suddenly, *Bam! Pow! Biff! Splatt!*

Two wet rags and two soggy sponges hit the boys on the backs of their necks, and when Wally and his brothers wheeled around, the Malloy girls were disappearing inside the house and the door slammed shut.

"That does it," said Jake. "We've got to do something. What's the scariest thing you can think of, Wally? We'll start with Beth. Have you thought of anything yet?"

And, as always, Wally said the first thing that came to mind: "Floating heads."

"Like we used to do with the Bensons on Halloween?" said Jake, his eyes lighting up. "Wally, it's wonderful! It's perfect!"

"Floating heads!" said Josh.

"Wow!" breathed Peter.

Eight

▼

Floating Heads

It was almost too delicious to think about. All through dinner that evening Wally tried not to smile, but whenever he caught Josh's or Jake's eye, he felt the corners of his mouth turning up just a bit at the edges.

"Well, how did the window cleaning go?" Mr. Hatford asked as he passed the peas.

"Went okay," said Josh.

"Did you get better acquainted with the Malloy girls?" asked their mother. "What are they like?"

"A Whomper, a Weirdo, and a Crazie," replied Peter.

"Just girls, Mom, that's all," Wally said quickly.

Mrs. Hatford helped herself to the ravioli in the center of the table. "Did Mrs. Malloy say anything more about my cake?"

"No. . . ."

Mom looked disappointed, Wally thought.

There was a little framed motto on the wall of the dining room: *If Mama ain't happy, ain't nobody happy,* it said. Maybe that was true of the Malloys as well. If the Malloy girls were unhappy here in Buckman, their mother wouldn't be happy either. And if Mrs. Malloy wasn't happy, she'd probably talk her husband into taking them back to Ohio. Wally hoped so, anyway.

But right now it was Mrs. Hatford who was unhappy.

"I had rather hoped—well, a cake like that wins ribbons in some places!" she said.

"First time you see her, she'll probably ask for the recipe," said Father. "*Nobody* makes chocolate chiffon cake the way you do, Ellen."

Wally went back to studying the ravioli on his plate. It was only recently Mother had tried anything fancy like ravioli. Usually, the people of Buckman stuck to fried chicken, beef pot-roasts, and pork chops with gravy. But someone had told Mrs. Hatford about the frozen ravioli you could buy at the grocery, and Wally was trying to figure out how they got the meat inside the little squares of dough. Did they make a pocket of dough first and then cut a little hole in the top and pour in the filling? Or did they put the meat between two pieces of dough, like a sandwich, and seal the edges together, or—

"Eat, Wally," said his father.

Wally quit studying the ravioli and thought about floating heads again. Last year at Halloween,

▲▼▲▼▲▼▲▼▲▼▲▼▲▼

when the Bensons were still here, the boys had frightened the residents of Buckman half to death with their floating heads.

It was the Bensons' idea, actually. Each boy bought a rubber mask, the scariest he could find, and each set out with a flashlight, long after tricks-or-treats were over for the evening, when children were settling down to count the pieces of candy they had collected and adults were turning off porch lights, glad that another Halloween was over. What each Benson and Hatford boy had done was sneak up to a lighted window, rap on the pane, then hold a flashlight beneath his chin so that the light illuminated the rubber mask and no more.

To a child looking up, or an adult turning around in his or her chair, all that could be seen in the dark outside was a grotesque head, made worse by the fact that the boy did not just stand there, but bobbed up and down, this way and that, so that it seemed for all the world as if a bodiless head were floating around outside the window. Children screeched, women screamed, and by the time anyone got to the door, the boys were halfway down the street, laughing to beat the band.

Jake had planned the details. They would wait until later, when Mother was working on her quilt and Dad was watching TV. Then they would creep outside with the zombie mask from last year, the worst of the lot, quietly place the ladder against the Malloys' house, just beneath Beth's window, and

Josh would climb up with the mask and flashlight, and rap.

"I know which window it is too," Josh had said. "When I was washing the windows, I found out where each girl sleeps. Eddie's got baseball stuff all over her walls, Caroline's got pictures of movie stars, and Beth's got books."

He sat down to draw a picture of Beth throwing up her hands in fright as she stared at a face outside her window. Josh had four sketchbooks full of drawings of all that the Hatfords had done with the Bensons when they lived in Buckman, and one of the favorite ways to spend a rainy day was to get out the sketches and remember how and where they had done each thing. Already, the boys discovered, Jake had a sketch of what Caroline might have looked like had she been eaten by fish, a picture of Eddie dumping her tray over Jake's head in the cafeteria, a sketch of the girls in the river trying to retrieve the plate, and a drawing of the girls and their mother right after the water fight.

Peter grinned as he studied the picture of Beth and the floating head. "Make her mouth open and her eyes look like *this!*" he said, demonstrating.

▼ ▼ ▼

After dinner the boys were strangely quiet, sitting around the living room pretending to watch TV with their father, their eyes on the clock. Sometimes Mr. Hatford fell asleep on the couch and slept right up until bedtime. Then he wouldn't know whether the boys were home or not. They could leave the TV on, and Mother, stitching her quilt upstairs, would think they were all in the living room.

To Wally's horror, however, Father suddenly reached over, turned off the TV, and stretched.

"Same old stuff, night after night," he said. "One of these evenings I think I'd like to walk over to the college and watch football practice—see what kind of a team we've got shaping up this year."

Jake and Josh exchanged glances.

"You'd have to go early, Dad, because I think they only practice until six-thirty," Wally said.

"I know. Maybe tomorrow. Think I'll go outside awhile, stretch my legs." He got up, put on a jacket, and went out on the porch.

"Hoo boy," said Josh. The boys followed him out, and walked beside him as he sauntered along the river.

"My favorite season," he said. "Used to walk along this very same path when I was just a little kid. Spent my whole life in this town, you know that?"

"Did you ever want to live anywhere else?" asked Wally.

"Noplace I could think of."

"So why did the Bensons leave?" asked Jake. "We thought *they* liked it here too."

"Hal Benson just wanted to try out another college—see if he liked teaching down in Georgia as much as he liked the school up here. Guess you have to try something to be sure." Father looked down at Wally, who was on his left side. "You miss those boys, don't you?"

"What do you think?" said Wally.

"Don't you figure it might be kinda fun to have a mess of girls around for a while?"

"You're joking," said Josh.

Even in the darkness Wally could tell that his dad was grinning a little. "I don't know, that young one's kind of cute. Something's a little wrong with her nose, though. Don't quite know what it is."

▼ ▼ ▼

About nine o'clock, Father was in the cellar, using the electric sander on an old dresser Mother wanted refinished, and she was upstairs working on her quilt, the radio going beside her.

Peter was supposed to have had his bath and be in bed, but because the boys had promised, they agreed to take him with them if they could get him out of the house unseen.

"We're going down to the bridge, Mom," Wally called to his mother. "Be back in a little while."

"Don't you go picking up poison ivy, now," Mrs. Hatford called, trying to hold a needle between her lips as she spoke, then running it through the quilt again.

"We won't. We'll stay on the path," Wally said.

There was no answer. Mother was humming along with the radio.

"C'mon," Wally whispered into Peter's room,

and the small boy tiptoed after them, his untied sneakers sticking out below his pajama bottoms.

They whispered all the way across the bridge, even though they didn't have to be quiet there. By the time they got to Island Avenue on the other side, they weren't saying anything at all. Josh had the green zombie mask with the gray eyes, Jake had the flashlight, and Wally and Peter were going along as lookouts.

It was a good thing the Malloys didn't have any dogs, Wally thought, because a dog would have heard them coming as soon as they crossed the bridge. As it was the boys kept to the shadows, and all strained to see if there was a light on in the right-hand bedroom above the front porch—Beth's room. There was. Wally and Jake poked each other and grinned. They crept up the side of the Malloys' driveway and opened the door of the garage.

Squeeeak! They froze in their tracks. All faces turned toward the house. But no one appeared at the windows, no one came to the door, and at last, convinced they were undetected, they picked up the long ladder, Wally at one end, Jake at the other, and carried it silently over to the bedroom in the corner.

Again they watched. Again they waited. Still no one came.

"Ready?" Jake whispered.

Josh nodded and slipped on the zombie mask. Wally sucked in his breath.

Flashlight in hand, Josh started up the rungs.

He was going as quietly as he could, Wally could tell, but even then the ladder seemed to make a kind of *pung, pung* sound with each step.

"Shhhh," warned Jake below. Josh stopped and waited. Nobody came. He went on.

Wally and his brothers watched. Josh stopped and adjusted the mask. He went up two more rungs until he was right outside Beth's window. At that very minute the light inside went out. And a second later, Josh's flashlight came on. He tapped, then bobbed up and down, this way and that.

There was a scream from inside—a cross between a train whistle and a fire alarm.

Whipping off his mask, Josh came down the ladder two rungs at a time.

They could hear Mr. Malloy yelling, "Beth? What's wrong?" Footsteps. More yelling. Voices.

The boys sprinted back down the driveway, watching the house over their shoulders. Wally faced forward again to see a baseball cap coming toward them, but there was no time to prevent a collision.

Wham! Crunch!

"Going somewhere?" came Eddie's voice.

"Yikes!" hollered Wally as a hand grabbed his shirt. He had never known that a tall, skinny girl could be so strong. She seemed to have Josh by the collar as well, dragging them both back toward the house. Wally wrestled free, but collided again, this time with Jake, and then he tripped over Peter. In the dark it was hard to see which arm belonged to whom.

"What are you guys up to anyway?" asked Eddie, but the boys got away and ran pell-mell to the bridge.

"You got the flashlight?" Jake asked Wally breathlessly.

"Heck, no. You were carrying it."

"I thought you grabbed it," Josh said. "*Some-one did!*"

But that someone was already inside the house.

Nine

▼

Ransom

Caroline was standing in the bathroom, practicing expressions in the mirror. She had actually been studying her eyebrows to see what they did when she went from sad to frightened, from scared to angry, and it was then she heard the scream.

Thinking her sister was being strangled, Caroline rushed into the room across the hall to find Beth on the floor, her chair overturned, eyes huge.

"What *is* it?" Caroline cried.

"Oh, Caroline, the most horrible thing right outside my window!"

"Girls, what's going on?" asked their father, hurrying in. Mother followed.

"Dad, there was something right outside my window!" Beth cried, still shaken.

"What was it?"

"A bobbing head. A floating face! It was green

with gray eyes, and . . . oh, it was awful! All decayed, with drool coming out of its mouth, and . . .''

Father reached down and picked up the book Beth had been reading: *The Creeping Dead.*

"Don't you think it's time you read something else for a change?"

"I only had half a chapter to go, and I just had to know how it ended," Beth said. "But what I saw wasn't my imagination; it was real!"

Caroline and her mother went to the window.

"Well, I don't see a thing," said Mrs. Malloy. "Eddie went next door to take back the eggs I borrowed. I'll bet it was her."

"It wasn't Eddie!" Beth declared.

"I'll go check," said Father.

He started down the stairs, the others behind him, just as Eddie came up.

"What's happening?" she asked.

"You missed a floating face," Caroline told her dryly. "Dad's going out to check."

"Don't bother," Eddie said. "Guess who I just bumped into? Crashed into, actually, they were in such a hurry to get away."

"*Them?*" cried Beth.

Eddie nodded.

"Who?" said Mother. "Those Hatford boys?"

"The very same," said Eddie. "There's a ladder up against the house, right under Beth's window."

"What now!" Mother exclaimed. "Those guys must drive their mother nuts."

Coach Malloy, however, was grinning. "That's the kind of thing you get when you have boys, Jean. Now, don't you go telling on them. They helped wash our windows, didn't they?"

Caroline waited as her parents went back downstairs, then she and Eddie went inside Beth's bedroom and shut the door.

"Those guys are terrible!" Beth said angrily.

"It could have been worse," said Caroline. "You could have been naked." Frankly, it had been a wonderful trick, Caroline decided, and she only wished that she had thought of it first to play on the boys.

"We've got to get even!" Beth declared. "We've just *got* to, Eddie!"

Eddie only smiled. "We already have. I've got their flashlight. A *good* flashlight too. I'll bet it belongs to their dad. They won't get it back unless they give us something in return."

"What?" asked Caroline.

"I haven't decided yet," said Eddie. "But believe me, they'll have to crawl!"

It would make such a marvelous story, Caroline thought. Sort of like Cinderella, only with the shoe on the other foot. This time *they* had the glass slipper, and whoever it belonged to had to come beg for it.

▼ ▼ ▼

On their way to school the next day Beth and Eddie showed Caroline the ransom note they had written to the Hatfords:

To whom it may concern:

If you ever hope to see your flashlight again, you will meet us at the swinging bridge at 7:30 this evening, and you will each say aloud, "I am honestly and truly sorry for the trouble I have caused, and will be a faithful, obedient servant of the realm, now and forever."

The Malloy Musketeers

"Servant of the realm?" Caroline asked. "What does that mean?"

"I don't know," said Beth, "but I read it in a book, and it sounded wonderful."

"It *is* wonderful!" said Caroline. "We could go walking down the path tonight single file, dressed like Egyptian princesses or something, and make them kneel down on one knee when they said it."

"Not me," said Eddie. "I'm not going as any princess."

"The boys would never do that," said Beth. "Getting them to say they're sorry is going to be hard enough."

"Who gets the note?" Caroline wanted to know.

"You're going to give it to Wally. If we gave it to

81

Jake or Josh, they wouldn't even read it—probably just make a spitball out of it," Eddie said.

Caroline could hardly wait to get to class. When the bell rang and she went in her room, however, Wally wouldn't even look at her, which told her just how upset the boys were that they had lost their father's flashlight.

She decided to wait until Miss Applebaum finished talking before she dropped the note over Wally's shoulder. But Miss Applebaum wouldn't shut up. She was talking about the invention of the telegraph or something, which did not interest Caroline in the least. Caroline rested her head on one hand and drew a picture of Miss Applebaum in her notebook.

The more the teacher droned on, the wilder the drawing became. She gave Miss Applebaum a monstrous mouth, with fire coming out of it. She gave her horns and a tail and scales like a dragon. The dragon lady even looked like Miss Applebaum—had the same kind of hair and the same kind of glasses. Clickety, clackety went the teacher's mouth, like a telegraph of its own.

Wally raised one hand to go to the bathroom and Miss Applebaum nodded that he could go.

Now, thought Caroline, while he was out of the room. She waited until Miss Applebaum was looking the other way, then quickly leaned forward and dropped the note onto Wally's desk.

When Wally came back, Miss Applebaum was

still carrying on, and Caroline was busily drawing claws on the teacher's hands and feet.

She saw Wally's head bend down over the desk as though he were looking at something, saw his arms move slightly as though he were unfolding a piece of paper, and then she watched as his ears turned from pink to red.

A few minutes later a small piece of paper came flying over Wally's shoulder and landed on her notebook. Caroline opened it.

Malloy Musketeers, it said. *Drop dead.*

The telegraph led to the telephone and the phonograph, and Caroline felt that she could not stand it another minute. This time *she* raised her hand to be allowed to go to the rest room, and when the teacher nodded, she tiptoed out. Once in the hallway she gave a big sigh of relief.

The girls' rest room was on the other side of the auditorium, and Caroline did a risky thing. Instead of going around she opened one of the great doors to the darkened room, took the four steps up onstage, and walked out to the middle, staring up at the rows of seats before her. Goose bumps rose on her arms.

Someday, she was sure, she would be here, with lights shining down on her, in a gorgeous costume, and she would dazzle the people of Buckman as they'd never been dazzled before. She walked to the very edge of the stage and whispered to the audience, "A faithful and obedient servant of the realm, now and forever." It sounded wonderfully mysterious and romantic. That done, she crossed over, went down the steps, and out the door on the other side.

All heads were bent over desks when Caroline came back into the room, and as she went down the aisle to her seat, Miss Applebaum said, "We are all writing a paragraph about what we think is the world's greatest invention, Caroline."

Thank goodness the lecture was over, Caroline thought, and reached for her pencil.

When she looked down at her notebook, however, she realized that the picture of Miss Applebaum was gone. There were little bits of paper around the three metal rings, as though a paper had been quickly snatched away. Her heart leapt. She stared up at the teacher, wondering if Miss Applebaum had come by and taken it.

But the teacher seemed completely undisturbed. Caroline stared at the back of Wally's head. *He* had taken it! He *must* have. When he came back from the rest room and walked by her desk, he must have seen what she was drawing. And somehow, when she was out of the room herself, he had managed to turn around and take the drawing.

When the papers were collected fifteen minutes later, Caroline was not even sure what she had written. And on the way out the door to recess, she poked Wally in the back. "You give me my paper or else," she said angrily.

Wally just smiled. "Meet me at the swinging bridge at seven-thirty this evening, and crawl down the path on your hands and knees," he said, and headed for the door.

Caroline was beside herself. This was blackmail! Beth and Eddie would never forgive her for doing something so stupid.

It was a horrible day, and as soon as school was out, Caroline charged out the door like a hornet and told Eddie and Beth what had happened. The Hatford boys had already headed for home, and were looking at the girls over their shoulders, laughing and hooting as they went.

When Caroline and her sisters reached the swinging bridge, Caroline was too angry to go home. Too angry to speak, almost. She stood glaring after the Hatford boys as they went up on the porch of their house and slammed the door. And then she saw something else: clothes drying on the clothesline in back of their house.

"Wait here," she told Beth and Eddie.

She marched right up on the Hatfords' lawn. Without looking to the right or left she stalked around to the back, grabbed a pair of Jockey shorts off the clothesline, then ran for her life as the boys came out on the porch and stared.

Waving the Jockey shorts high in the air, she tore across the swinging bridge, Beth and Eddie behind her, and didn't stop until they were safely in their house and up in Caroline's room.

"Wonderful!" said Eddie.

"I'll show them all around school!" Caroline declared. "I'll tell everyone in my class they're Wally's. 'How are your Munsingwears today?' I'll ask him. He and his brothers don't get back their flashlight *or* shorts until they return my drawing of Miss Applebaum *and* get down on one knee and apologize."

The phone rang.

"I'll bet they want to exchange things right now," Beth said, giggling, as the girls dashed out in the hall. "They can't even wait until evening."

Caroline picked up the phone. "Malloy Musketeers, Caroline speaking."

There was a short pause at the other end. And then a man's voice said, "Caroline, this is Mr. Hatford, across the river. I wonder if you would mind returning my briefs."

Ten

▼

Siren Song

Wally, Josh, Jake, and Peter stood still as cement as their father made the phone call.

Mr. Hatford turned around, phone in hand.

"She says she'll return my briefs if you return her paper, Wally. Do you know what she's talking about?"

Wally nodded and swallowed. "Tell her I'll return the paper if she returns the flashlight."

Mr. Hatford spoke into the phone again. "He says he'll return the paper if you return the flashlight. Don't ask me what's going on around here. I'm only their father. . . . Okay, five minutes from now on the bridge. . . . He'll be there."

Wally's father put down the telephone and looked at the boys. "That wouldn't be *my* flashlight she's talking about, would it?"

Wally nodded still again.

"Is this what goes on in the afternoons when

I'm not here? People run off with my flashlight and shorts? I get home early for the first time in a couple of months, and what do I see? Some girl leaving our yard at sixty miles an hour waving my underwear in the wind!"

"She's the Crazie," Peter explained soberly.

"Well, if you've got something of hers, Wally, you get on out to the bridge and give it back. I want my briefs and my flashlight back, and anything else that's missing. What do they want next? Socks? Toothbrush? Keys? They holding a garage sale or something?"

Wally went to his room for Caroline's drawing of Miss Applebaum.

"You guys have to come too," he murmured to the others, and they all followed him out the door.

For a minute or so they trudged silently across the yard and over to the other side of the road.

"Once we get Dad's stuff back, we'll be even," Wally said, thinking that this would be a good time to forget about the Malloys once and for all.

"But we can't stop now!" said Jake. "If we're not bugging the girls, what *will* we do?"

That was something Wally hadn't thought about. "Mom will enroll us in violin lessons," he said worriedly.

"She'll make us get a paper route," said Josh.

"She'll send us to camp next summer," said Peter.

▲▼▲▼▲▼▲▼▲▼▲▼▲▼

Jake grinned. "So we've got to stay busy, right?"

"Right," said Wally.

The boys looked at each other and smiled.

"Tell you what," said Josh. "We won't start anything if *they* don't."

"Yeah," said Jake. "But they will."

Caroline and her sisters were coming across the bridge. Wally knew that his dad was back on the porch watching, and he wasn't about to do anything dumb like float Caroline's paper over the edge of the cable railing.

Caroline's face was red. He had never seen her embarrassed before, but he was looking at it now.

"Here's your paper," he muttered.

"Here's your stuff," said Caroline, and handed him a sack.

Eddie and Beth looked daggers at all four boys together.

"You better check that sack," whispered Josh as the boys turned and started back again. "They probably took the batteries out of the flashlight."

Wally looked in the sack. Everything was there. He checked the flashlight. Two batteries, one bulb. He took out the briefs and turned them over. No writing on the seat of the pants.

"Thank you," said their father when they reached the porch. "Now, do you think it's possible that you boys can stay out of trouble for a couple of days? If you want something to do, you could wash *our* windows, not to mention my car or the dishes or the kitchen floor."

"I've got homework," said Jake.

"Me too," said Wally, and all four boys went upstairs.

▼ ▼ ▼

There was always a "Back-to-School" night in Buckman the second week of September. No matter what, every parent who had a child in school was supposed to go to his or her classroom that night, meet the teacher, sit in the kid's seat, and listen to a talk about what the students would be learning that year. Afterward there were cookies and coffee in the gym, and the principal went around shaking hands. You no more missed Back-to-School night in Buckman than you missed your grandmother's funeral.

Mr. Hatford was going to spend the evening in Josh and Jake's classroom, while Mrs. Hatford would divide the evening between Miss Applebaum and Peter's teacher. The boys, of course, would stay at home.

Always before, on Back-to-School night, the Hatfords went to the Bensons', or the Bensons came to the Hatfords', and the boys wrestled on the rug, made popcorn, ate candy, enjoying the fact that for once they were free and their folks were in school.

But this time there were no Bensons to come over, and to make matters worse, it rained.

"We could go through the kitchen and eat all the chocolate chips," said Wally.

"There aren't any, I already looked," Jake told him.

"We could call up some of the guys at school to come over," said Josh.

"Who do we like at school?" Jake asked. There were friends, of course, but none they liked as well as the Bensons.

"We could wrap up in blankets and roll down the stairs," said Peter.

"Negative," said Josh.

They decided at last to turn out all the lights and play hide and seek. Wally was it.

He sat down on the couch in the living room and counted to fifty.

"Here I come, ready or not," he yelled, and groped his way to the hall.

It was one of the most exciting games the boys played, and they reserved it for moments of incredible boredom. When you were "it" in the dark you never knew when a hand was going to reach out and grab you, whether you would crawl under the bed and find a body, whether you would collide with someone on the stairs.

He heard a soft thud from somewhere, but wasn't quite sure if it was up or down, in or out. It had to be in, though, because outside was off-limits. There were three live bodies waiting to be found, and in the dark, they could change hiding places as much as they liked. Even if you touched something, you had to make sure it was a person.

The noise came again. Upstairs. Wally was sure of that now. He ran his hand along the wall and started up, his other hand sweeping the air in front of him.

Halfway up the stairs, however, he heard another sound, and this time goose bumps rose on his arms. It was a sound like nothing he had ever heard before.

It seemed to be half human, half animal, yet more like a fire siren, only very, very soft. It rose and fell like the wind. Maybe it *was* the wind.

Then it stopped, and all Wally heard was the rain beating down on the roof. He went on, running his hand along the wall, poking each step with his foot to make sure there wasn't a hand ready to grab his ankle. Just as he got to the top, however, the strange siren song came again.

He heard somebody running along the hallway, and then Peter's voice, calling shakily, "Wally?"

"What's the matter?" Wally said, putting out his other hand so Peter wouldn't run into him. Peter ran into him anyway, and grabbed his arm.

"What's that noise?" Peter said.

"I don't know. Probably Jake or Josh."

"I don't wanna play this game anymore," Peter told him.

"Well, go down and sit on the couch, then, until I find the other guys."

"No, I wanna stay by you."

Whoooeeeoooo. Whoooeeeoooo.

It was not a siren. It was not anything Wally could figure out.

"Josh, cut it out," he yelled.

"It's not me," came a voice from one of the bedrooms. "What the heck is it?"

"Jake, I'll bet."

"Turn on the lights," Peter begged.

"No, we can't until we find Jake. That's the rule."

Whoooeee, whoooeee, whoooeeeoooo. . . .

Footsteps downstairs.

"Hey, what are you guys doing?" came Jake's voice. "Who's singing that song?"

It was *not* Jake. Three sets of feet went flying down the stairs, the boys tumbling and rolling, until Wally and his brothers lay in a heap at the bottom.

Eleven

▼

Trapped

Three figures huddled on the widow's walk on top of the Hatfords' house. Rain beat steadily down on their yellow slickers and the air was cold.

"Even if we catch pneumonia and die, it's worth it," said Caroline, her teeth chattering.

"Even if we fall off the roof and break both legs," Eddie agreed.

"One more time?" Beth asked.

"No. Didn't you hear them running? Let's wait until we think they've forgotten about it, then sock it to them again," said Eddie. They giggled.

It had all started when Beth heard a group of women called Sweet Honey in the Rock on the radio, singing a song they had written called "Emergency." She had called the others to listen. Caroline wasn't sure how they did it, but, using only their voices, the singers had managed to make themselves sound just like a fire siren, each singing a different pitch, but rising and falling together at exactly the same time.

So Caroline, Beth, and Eddie had gone out in the garage and lain in the loft, practicing quietly, and they did it—not as well as Sweet Honey in the Rock, but well enough. What's more, they discovered that if they kept their voices soft, and wavered them just a little, they sounded like something none of them had ever heard before—not a siren, exactly —not quite human, not quite animal. . . . And as soon as they discovered that, they knew what they were going to do. Never had they felt such power.

"How long should we wait? I'm so soggy, I'm going to grow mushrooms," Beth said.

"We have to lull them into thinking they were imagining things," Eddie told her.

Caroline smiled to herself in the dark as she huddled in her corner of the widow's walk. She had been so embarrassed when Mr. Hatford called and asked for his briefs back! And then, to have to walk down to the bridge with Mr. Hatford watching, and exchange things with Wally—it was too much; a humiliation that dreadful needed revenge.

She almost wished it were daylight and clear so that she could see out over Buckman. It felt strange being up here on the Hatfords' roof at night, and she imagined how much fun the boys must have had spying on her and her sisters when her family first moved in. If she and Eddie and Beth had lived over here, and it were the *Hatfords* moving in, she had no doubt they would have been spying on *them*. But that was beside the point. She wasn't even sure *what* the point was anymore, except that she and Beth and Eddie had never had so much excitement back in Ohio, and she hoped they would not go back when a year was over.

"Okay, let's do it again," Eddie whispered.

All three girls leaned down over the trapdoor in the roof, mouths close against the crack.

"One, two, three . . . go," said Beth.

And then they sang the song—the terrible, electrifying siren song that started low and soft, then rose higher and higher, louder and louder, tapering off into nothing, like the wind.

There was the thud of running feet once more from inside. Closet doors opening and closing. Yells. Squares of yellow light appeared on the lawn as lights went on all over the house.

"We're driving them absolutely nuts." Eddie grinned.

"Positively bonkers," said Caroline. "How long are we going to keep doing this? Till they come running and screaming out of the house with their hands up?"

It was a question they hadn't discussed.

"Why don't we keep it up till their parents get home?" said Beth.

"Because then *our* parents will be home, and we'll have a lot of explaining to do," said Eddie.

"What time is it?"

Eddie tried to see her watch in the darkness. "Eight-thirty, I think."

"Fifteen more minutes, then," Caroline said. "Mom said not to expect them back before nine. That will give us time to get home and put the ladder away."

The footsteps and door banging went on for some time before the house grew quiet again. Once more Beth gave the signal, and once more the three girls leaned over, noses almost touching the roof, and made the sound that rose and fell like the wind. This time they wavered their voices, so that the song was even more eerie—ghostlike.

When they stopped, however, there was no noise from below. No voices, no footsteps. Nothing. The girls did it again, a little louder, and waited. Still nothing. Caroline looked over the side of the railing. There were no squares of yellow light on the lawn, meaning that the boys had turned out all the lights. What were they doing?

She and Eddie and Beth exchanged glances.

"Maybe they left. Maybe they just silently closed up and headed for the school to get their parents," said Beth.

"Wouldn't that be a *blast*!" said Eddie.

"We could do this again sometime, when their folks are away," Beth laughed. "We could drive them *wild*."

"We could drive *them* out of Buckman, and

then we'd have the town to ourselves," said Caroline.

They waited a few minutes longer. If the boys *had* gone to the school to get their parents, it meant the Hatfords' car could be turning in at any moment.

"We'd better go," said Eddie.

Carefully they climbed over the side of the widow's walk, then made their way down the sloping roof, scooting along on the seat of their pants—slowly, cautiously, grasping the shingles with their fingertips as they came, Caroline in the lead. But when she reached the place they had left the ladder, Caroline saw that the ladder was gone.

"WHOEEEOOO!" came a yell from the yard below, and the four Hatford brothers emerged from the porch, yelling like banshees in the darkness.

For the second time Caroline's face burned with humiliation. There was nothing left but surrender.

"Okay, okay, put the ladder back up," she said, but the boys paid no attention.

"WHOEEEOOOO!" they yelped, running about the yard in the rain.

"Put that ladder back up!" Eddie commanded, as though it would do any good.

"You wanted to be up there, you're up there," yelled Jake. "Have a good time."

"Want some pillows? Have a good sleep!" called Josh.

It was beginning to rain harder now. It came

down in huge drops, like water splashing out of a basin.

"Wally!" bellowed Caroline, but the boys only laughed and ducked under the porch roof. What had been fun before was scary now. Because of the rain and the dark, it was hard to maneuver.

"Come on," said Beth, inching her way back up the roof. "I've got an idea."

Caroline and Eddie followed clumsily, strands of wet hair blowing in their faces. Caroline felt wet through and through. They reached the railing around the widow's walk and crawled under.

"I just have a hunch. . . ." Beth said, bending over the trapdoor again. "Help me lift it, Eddie. See if it's latched."

All three girls edged their fingers beneath the rim of the lid to the trapdoor and tugged. Just as Beth suspected, the boys hadn't latched it again after their last spying episode.

The girls stared down into total darkness.

"Are there stairs?" Eddie asked.

Caroline leaned over and put one arm down as far as it would reach. "No," she said disappointedly.

"We could jump," said Eddie.

"We don't dare. We don't know what's under there."

"What good is this going to do?" Eddie said.

"Just wait," Beth told her. "We're going to keep the door open. You'll see."

There was hail along with the rain now—smaller stones at first, then larger and larger.

"WHOOOOEEEEOOOO!" yelled the boys delightedly on the porch below.

"Let's go inside where it's warm and dry," came Jake's voice loudly from the porch.

"Yeah, let's make some hot chocolate," said Wally.

"With marshmallows," added Peter. "Yum, yum!"

There was the sound of a door slamming as the boys went back in.

A minute went by. Then two or three. The rain and hail was hitting the floor beneath the trapdoor. The girls could hear it.

Suddenly a light came on, illuminating the Hatfords' attic and the stepladder beneath. Hail was pinging against the floor. There was already a large puddle of water.

"Hey!" came Wally's voice. "Jake! They've opened the trap! They're letting in water!"

Feet pounded on the stairs, and Caroline looked down into Josh's and Jake's angry faces.

"Close the trap!" Jake demanded. "You'll ruin the floor."

"So?" said Caroline.

A car was pulling in the driveway.

"Your folks are home," said Eddie.

"Come on down! Get out of here! Hurry up!" Josh yelled.

Caroline slid inside, holding on to the raised edge around the opening of the trap until her feet were securely on top of the stepladder. Eddie came next, and finally Beth, pulling the door closed behind her.

"Hurry!" Josh was saying, pushing them toward the stairs to the second floor, and they thundered down, the boys at their heels.

But it was too late. Just as Caroline reached the front door, it opened, and Mr. and Mrs. Hatford walked in.

"Hello," said Caroline, and then, as she and her sisters went outside, "Good-bye."

Twelve

▼

Letters

Mr. Hatford looked at his wife.

"Was it just my imagination, or did I see three girls, in yellow raincoats, walk out our front door?"

"You did," said Wally's mother. "Listen, you guys, what in the world is going on?"

"Those girls were up on our roof," Wally said.

"In *this* rain?"

"They were, Mom," Josh put in.

"Singing!" added Peter, nodding his head.

Mr. Hatford looked slowly around the room. "Singing in the rain; three girls in yellow raincoats; nine o'clock at night; on the roof."

"How did they get up there?" asked Mother.

"They brought a ladder," said Peter.

Wally wished his younger brother hadn't said that, because he knew what the next question would be. It was his father who asked and answered it both.

▲▼▲▼▲▼▲▼▲▼▲▼

"If they got *up* the ladder to get to the roof, why didn't they go *down* the ladder to get to the ground? Because the boys took the ladder away, why else?"

Wally wanted to sneak off to the living room with his brothers, but Father was in the doorway.

Mother sighed. "I used to think the Benson boys were more than I could take, but those girls are going to drive me wild. I wonder if the Malloys give any thought at all to how they are raising their children."

"Now, Ellen, we saw George and Jean Malloy at the school tonight, and they seemed warm and friendly to me," Father told her.

"Not friendly enough to tell me they liked my cake," Mother said huffily. "I gave them every opportunity, and all they talked about was how nice it was for the boys to wash their windows." She took off her jacket and hung it up. "Even sent the plate back without anything on it, a crack in it too. That's just not the way we do things in Buckman."

Wally ducked sheepishly under his father's arm and made his escape.

A letter arrived the following day from the Benson boys addressed to J.J.W. and P. Hatford:

Hi, Guys!
It's raining down here, so we figured it was time to write you all a letter. How ya doing?

We're doing okay, I guess. You know what Georgia's full of? Red ants. Red ants and roaches and lots of peach and pecan trees, and, of course, sun.

We've got this big old house—really, really old—near the University, and so far Dad likes it here. Mom too. She likes this house. It's got this enormous attic you wouldn't believe. If you guys were down here we'd be up in the attic all the time, I'll bet. Stuff's hidden in the walls—old newspapers and things, I mean. One of them dates back to 1887. Mom said the house used to belong to a Confederate soldier. We've been looking for bullets and stuff at the back of the yard, but so far we haven't found any.

Did Wally get Applebaum this year? You should see the teacher Danny got. A Georgia P-E-A-C-H. Every guy who gets her this year is one lucky stiff. School's not too bad. Lots of boys here, right in our neighborhood, too, so that's good. Wish you were here, though.

The first thing we'd do if you ever come down to Georgia is go up to the attic, because it's probably the first thing you'd want to see.

The second thing would be to ride around town on the tour bus. Boy, there's so much to do you could probably live here twenty years and not do it all.

Anyway, write to us sometime and tell us about the people who moved into our house. Mom wants to know if they're taking good care of it. I asked her the other day if we were going back to Buckman after the year is up, and she said she didn't know, it was up to Dad. So I asked him, and he said, "Who knows?"

Take care, you guys,
Bill
(and Danny and Steve and Tony and Doug)

Dear Bill (and Danny and Steve and Tony and Doug):

We got your letter and I can't say we're glad you like Georgia, because we hoped you wouldn't. You want to know who rents your house? A Whomper, a Weirdo, and a Crazie, that's who. So far here is what these girls have done:

1. Outpitched the boys at recess (even Jake).

2. Pretended one of their sisters (the Crazie) was dead and dumped her in the river.

3. Threw a cake in the river.

4. Stole a flashlight.

5. Stole Dad's underwear.

6. Crawled up on our roof in a rainstorm and hollered through our trapdoor.

If you were here, and we were in Georgia, would you be glad? I don't care if you guys have a Georgia P-E-A-C-H for a teacher or not. I don't care if you have Miss America. If you don't come back and send these dweebs back to Ohio, I'll tell everyone in Buckman how you wet your pants once on the playground.

Wally
(and Jake and Josh and Peter)
P.S. I don't know if the Malloys are taking good care

of your house or not. We had to go over and wash their windows for them. That should tell you something.

"I'll bet they're never coming back," Wally said as he sealed his letter.

"They sure didn't sound very sad about being in Georgia," said Josh.

"You know what?" said Jake after a minute. "If one of the Malloy girls ever comes over here again, let's kidnap her. Lock her up. We'll make her sisters pay plenty to get her back."

"Wow!" said Peter.

Thirteen

▼

Kidnapped

"**T**om and Ellen Hatford seem like such nice people," Mother said at breakfast as she put some melon on the table. "Did I tell you girls that we talked with them a little while at the school the other night? I told them I appreciated the boys helping wash our windows."

"Yeah, great job," Eddie said dryly.

"Mrs. Hatford, though, is . . . well, a bit on the odd side. I was standing with her over by the refreshment table, and as I reached for a cookie, she said she was glad my family enjoyed desserts so much, that we all had such hearty appetites. One little cookie, and she made it sound as though the five of us could finish off a whole cake in one meal! Strange."

"Very," agreed Eddie.

▼ ▼ ▼

At school that morning Caroline did not cross the auditorium to get to the rest room as she had been doing once a day since she had discovered the new route. The sixth-graders were in the auditorium watching a film, so it was not till lunchtime that, when Caroline peeked, it was dark and empty once again.

She did not have any trouble finding opportunities to step up on the stage. She could count on being excused from class at least once a day to go to the rest room. Sometimes she came in the building at recess to get a drink, and made an auditorium detour going back out again. If all else failed, she hurriedly ate her lunch and then—when she took her milk carton to the trash—simply walked on out the door into the hall, slipped into the auditorium, and, when she was finished, out the other side and onto the playground.

She'd gotten into the habit of taking a book in with her, any book at all, so she could practice reading a few paragraphs, with expression, from the stage. She could not talk nearly as loud as she would have liked, of course, because someone outside might hear, so she stage-whispered the paragraphs, always choosing a selection where at least two different people were speaking, to give her practice reading several parts.

The day before, she had read a selection from *Charlotte's Web*, where the spider confessed to eating other insects:

". . . I have to live, don't I?"

"Why, yes, of course," said Wilbur. "Do they taste good?"

"Delicious. Of course, I don't really eat them. I drink them—drink their blood. I love blood," said Charlotte, and her pleasant, thin voice grew even thinner and more pleasant.

Caroline had loved playing the part of Charlotte, and had practiced hard to make her voice "thin and pleasant." Pleasant was easy enough to do, but she'd had to work some to make it sound thin. The day before that she had read from *Alice in Wonderland:*

"But I don't want to go among mad people," Alice remarked.

"Oh, you can't help that," said the Cat: "we're all mad here. I'm mad. You're mad."

"How do you know I'm mad?" said Alice.

"You must be," said the Cat, "or you wouldn't have come here."

When she had found that passage in the book, she had thought all morning about how she should read the part of the Cheshire Cat. But today she had chosen a page from *The Wind in the Willows*, because it said that Mole spoke "in anguish of heart." All during arithmetic that morning she had wondered what sort of an expression "anguish of heart"

would be. Something very dramatic, she was sure—
a mixture of fear and sorrow, perhaps.

So when she went to throw out her milk carton
in the trash after eating, she sneaked across the hall
to the auditorium and, with the book tucked under
her shirt, slipped up onstage, out from behind the
thick velvet curtain, and directly to the center of the
platform.

This was a conversation between Ratty and
Mole. Caroline decided that she would look to the
left when she was reading the part of Mole, and to
the right when she was reading Ratty. She cleared
her throat and began:

The call was clear, the summons was plain.
He must obey it instantly, and go. "Ratty!" he
called, full of joyful excitement, "hold on! Come
back! I want you quick!"

"Oh, *come* along, Mole, do!" replied the Rat
cheerfully, still plodding along.

"Please stop, Ratty!" pleaded the poor Mole,
in anguish of heart. "You don't understand! It's
my home, my old home! I've just come across the
smell of it, and it's close by here, really quite
close. And I *must* go to it, I must, I must! Oh,
come back, Ratty! Please, please come back!"

Caroline stiffled a sob.
There was a titter in the audience.
The audience?

110

▲▼▲▼▲▼▲▼▲▼▲▼▲▼

Caroline's hand dropped, the book in it, and she stared hard into the darkness of the auditorium.

The laughter came again, louder this time, and quickly became a loud guffaw.

The next thing Caroline knew, Wally and some of the other fourth-grade boys were charging down the aisle and out the side door, yelling:

"Oh, please come back!"

"I *must* go, I *must*!"

And suddenly there was Miss Applebaum in the doorway, peering into the auditorium.

"Caroline?" she said.

Caroline walked stiffly offstage.

"What's going on in here?" the teacher asked. "You're supposed to be out on the playground."

"I was just leaving," Caroline said, and without looking in a mirror, she knew that her cheeks—her whole face, in fact—was flaming.

Out on the grass Wally and the other boys were doubled over. They reeled in laughter, fell against each other, and one boy lay on his back, screaming, "The smell of it! You don't understand! Oh, come back, Ratty! Please, please do!"

▼ ▼ ▼

Caroline did not tell her sisters what had happened in the auditorium. It was too embarrassing. They hadn't even known she was sneaking into the auditorium at all. She could think of nothing else the rest of the day, and wondered how long the boys had been there. It was Wally, she was sure, who had led them all there, but had they been spying on her at other times as well?

Had he been there the day she'd played tearful Becky Thatcher, lost in the cave with Tom Sawyer, and crying, *Tom, Tom, we're lost! we're lost!*

What she decided was that she would pay Wally back for this humiliation. This was a hundred times worse than stealing Mr. Hatford's shorts. Day in, day out, noontime, nighttime, she didn't care, somehow, someway, she would catch *him* doing something as embarrassing as being caught onstage had been for her.

For the next few days Caroline said nothing at all to Wally Hatford, but she scarcely took her eyes off him. She followed him at a distance on the playground at recess. She stared when he went to the front of the room to put a problem on the blackboard. She watched from the next table when he ate his lunch. One false move from Wally Hatford, and she'd never let him forget it.

Just let her catch him with something yucky between his teeth. Just let her catch him with his pants unzipped. Let her catch *him* drawing something crazy in his notebook. *Wally Hatford*, she recited every morning, *your time will come.*

▼ ▼ ▼

Sunday was a clear day, warm and dry, and on days like this, the Hatford boys usually played in their backyard after church, once their clothes were changed. Walking along the river, Caroline and her sisters had often seen them whooping it up, playing kickball or throwing horseshoes.

Mr. and Mrs. Malloy had left early that morning for the funeral of a friend back in Ohio, and wouldn't be home until night. Caroline realized that if she could hide herself somewhere near the Hatfords' house, she could spy on Wally all day without being missed. She told her sisters this much: "Wally embarrassed me awful in school on Friday, and I'm going to get back at him no matter what."

Beth was sprawled in a chair on the lawn reading *The Shadow of the Werewolf*. "Don't start anything till I finish this book," she said.

"Well, I'm taking lunch with me, and I may not be home for a long time," Caroline said. "I just wanted you to know."

"What have you got in the sack?"

"Marshmallows and cheese crackers."

"Toss me a marshmallow?" Beth said, holding out her hands, then popped it in her mouth and returned to her book.

Caroline set out just before the Hatfords were due home from church. She remembered having seen a shed in the back of their house when she had snatched Mr. Hatford's underwear from the line. This, she decided, was where she would hide, and had no trouble getting the door open and closing it after her.

Once inside, she wished she'd brought a pillow

or something, because the shed was dusty, with a bare earth floor, and crammed with hoes and shovels, lawn mower and sprinkler.

There was, however, a narrow space between the edge of the door where the hinges were and the rest of the shed, and Caroline found that by sitting on an old toolbox and putting her eye to the crack, she could see almost the entire yard.

The Hatfords' Chevy was just pulling into the driveway, and the boys got out and walked single-file to the house. They all looked stiff and weird in their Sunday shirts and ties, and Caroline smiled as she dug into her sack of cheese crackers, and settled herself more comfortably on the toolbox.

She had expected it would be an hour at least before the boys ate dinner and came out in the yard, but was surprised when Mr. and Mrs. Hatford stepped out instead, dressed in old clothes, and carrying some empty baskets.

"Are you *sure* you don't want to come to the orchard with us?" Mother said, turning to Wally and Josh in the doorway.

"No way!" Josh told her. "You pick the apples and we'll eat 'em."

"We'll pick the apples, and you boys are going to help peel them," Mrs. Hatford replied. "Two bushels of apples would take me two days, but with six of us working, I figure we could do it in a couple of hours."

"Oh, Mom, not that!" Wally complained.

"You won't groan when you see my apple pies," his mother said, getting in the car. "Don't forget your sandwiches, now. They're on the counter." And the car backed down the drive.

Caroline watched as Jake, Josh, Wally, and Peter came out the back door and sat on the steps to eat their sandwiches. They talked about how far you could shoot with a BB gun, and which decayed first after you died, your teeth or your bones.

They were too far away for Caroline to catch every word, but she wished the boys would tell a story on Wally—something embarrassing he had done. She'd tell it around at school, and Wally would wonder how she knew.

When the boys had finished eating, Josh brought out a sketchbook of some kind, and seemed to be drawing funny pictures in it, because the boys were all laughing.

"That's her, all right!" she heard Wally hoot. "That's just how she looked up there onstage, holding her book out in front of her like that. Yeah, make the corners of her mouth turn down, Josh, like she's about to bawl."

Caroline's cheeks flamed a second time. Josh was drawing a picture of her! Wally must have told them all about listening to her up onstage.

"Write what she's saying, Josh," Wally continued. " 'Oh, come back, Ratty! Please, please do!' " He mimicked her in a high voice, and the boys howled, Peter loudest of all.

It was all Caroline could do to keep from bursting out of the toolshed right that minute and pounding Wally on the head. She wouldn't be surprised if he had told it at the dinner table in front of his parents. Now the boys were looking at other pictures in the sketchbook, and from their hoots and laughter, Caroline could tell that Josh had sketched other pictures of her and her sisters as well.

When the laughter died away at last, Wally came out into the yard with a small rubber ball and practiced catching by bouncing it against the shed.

Blang! Blang! Blang! Caroline's head began to pound. Each time the ball hit the metal shed it sounded like an explosion in a tin-can factory. On and on it went—at least twenty minutes. Caroline felt as though her head would split.

Finally Wally stopped, and all four boys lay down on their backs in the grass.

"What do you want to do?" Wally asked Josh.

"I don't know," said Josh. "What do you want to do?"

"Go to the school and shoot some baskets?" asked Jake.

"Naw," said Wally.

"Bug the girls?" asked Josh.

"Yeah!" said Peter, Jake, and Wally.

Ha! thought Caroline.

"We'd better wait awhile, they're probably having Sunday dinner," Josh told them.

"Man!" said Jake. "I've thought of all *kinds* of stuff we could do to them at Halloween!"

"Yeah?" Caroline heard Josh say. "Wait till it *snows*! Boy, will we ever get them then."

"You remember how we used to sneak out on New Year's Eve with the Bensons, and Bill would blow his cornet right under someone's window at midnight? Wouldn't old Caroline flip?" said Wally.

"What about firecrackers?" said Peter. "We could put firecrackers in tin cans and set them on the Malloys' porch."

"They haven't even seen Smuggler's Cove yet."

"We could throw Eddie's dumb cap down the old coal mine, see if she'd crawl in after it. Bet she would too," Jake said. "Remember when Tony Benson crawled in there and the rescue squad had to get him out?"

"Wait till we get to junior high school. There are about a hundred things you can do to a girl's locker. We could wait until Beth put her coat in some morning, and then fix it so she couldn't get the lock open." Josh's voice.

"Ha! Put *Caroline* in a locker and keep her there all weekend!"

More laughter.

Back in the toolshed Caroline smiled to herself. This was even better than she'd thought. Here she was, hearing all their plans! Wait till she told her sisters. They'd know everything the boys were going to do before they did it. No matter what the boys tried, the girls would be ready. This was far more fun than Ohio!

"Wait till the town picnic next summer. Man, we'll beat the girls at *every*thing," said Jake. "The relay race, the sack race, the three-legged race . . ."

". . . the skateboard contest . . ."

". . . the pie-eating contest . . ."

". . . volleyball."

There was a long silence then, and for a moment Caroline thought the boys might have gone inside. She put her eye to the crack again. They were still on the grass.

"Unless . . ." Wally said, and Jake finished for him.

". . . they go back to Ohio."

"Yeah," said Josh. "If the Bensons come back, it's over."

More silence.

"You know what I wish?" said Wally. "I hope the Bensons stay in Georgia long enough for us to do everything we've planned to do to the Malloys, and then come back."

"Yeah," said Jake. "That would be perfect."

"A year and a half, maybe," said Josh.

"Right," said Wally.

"Let's play horseshoes for a while," Jake suggested. He got to his feet and started straight toward the shed.

No! He was coming here! Caroline scrambled off

the toolbox, grabbing her lunch sack, and tried to hide behind the lawn mower.

The footsteps grew louder, then the sound of the hinges creaking as the door to the toolshed opened partway. Caroline saw Jake's hand reach inside for the horseshoes on one shelf. She flattened herself against the back wall, but it was no use. Jake saw.

"What . . . ?" His eyes opened wide. "Hey, guys, look what we caught!" Jake grinned as he opened the door wider. The others came running.

"It's Caroline!" said Peter.

"Spying on us!" cried Wally.

And before Caroline could scramble back over the lawn mower and make her escape, Jake slammed the door shut.

"Bring me the bicycle padlock, Wally!" he yelled. "We've got a hostage, and her sisters aren't getting her back without a ransom!"

Kidnapped!

Fourteen

▼

Hornswoggled

Wally and his brothers could not believe their good fortune! Caroline Malloy, trapped in the toolshed, and their parents away picking apples.

"We got her! We got her!" Peter sang, dancing around the yard. And then he stopped. "What's a hostage, Wally?"

"A person you keep prisoner until somebody pays to get her back," Wally told him. But then the enormity of what had happened began to sink in on him. How could this be? Only a few minutes ago he and his brothers were lying on their backs talking about Halloween and New Year's, and suddenly Caroline Malloy was a prisoner in their toolshed!

"Man, they aren't going to believe what we're going to make them say to get her back, are they, Jake?" Josh was saying. "What was it they wanted us to promise to get our flashlight back?"

"I am honestly and truly sorry for the trouble I

have caused, and .... something about an obedient servant of the realm," said Wally.

"They are going to *crawl*!" said Jake. "They are going to *creep*! They are going to *beg*! We're going to rub their noses in the dirt before we give their sister back. You hear that, Caroline?" he yelled.

There was no answer from the toolshed.

"Probably crying," said Peter. He looked around a little worriedly.

"You crying, Caroline?" asked Josh.

"Hoo boy, can she cry! You ought to see her up there onstage! The tears just pour," Wally put in.

"Well, we didn't make her go in the shed," said Josh.

"Right!" said Peter. "She went in there all by herself, didn't she, Wally?"

"How are we going to get a note to her sisters, though, without her parents finding out?" Wally wondered. "What if her folks start looking for her?"

"Then we've got to reach Beth and Eddie before they do. We'll say something about how we found her on our property," Jake decided.

"Yeah! Trespassing!" said Wally. "That's a crime, isn't it?"

"We could call the police!" Peter whooped.

"Her sisters will come and get her, you'll see," said Jake. "Come on. Let's write the note."

The boys went over to the back steps and sat down. Wally got a pencil and paper, and Jake dictated: " 'To whom it may concern . . .' "

" 'Namely, Whomper and Weirdo,' " added Josh.

" '. . . Caroline the Crazie was found spying on our property, and is now being held prisoner in our toolshed.' "

Wally wrote it down.

" 'If you tell anybody,' " Jake continued, " 'we will tell your folks all the stuff you've done so far to us. If you want to see Caroline again, you've got to crawl over to our house on your hands and knees . . .' "

" 'Lick our shoes . . .' " said Josh.

"They'll never do that," said Wally, "not even for Caroline."

"Okay. 'Crawl over to our house on your hands and knees and say, *We are honestly and truly sorry for the trouble we have caused, and . . .*' " Jake paused again.

" '*Will be your obedient servants. . . .*' " said Josh.

"No. Obedient slaves," said Jake. "That's it. '*We are honestly and truly sorry for the trouble we have caused, and will be your obedient slaves forever.*' "

"Perfect," said Josh.

Wally started to write it, then stopped. "I can't imagine Eddie saying 'your obedient slave forever.' "

"Yeah," said Josh gloomily. "I can't imagine them crawling on their hands and knees either."

"Well, they thought *we* would say something

like this!" Jake reminded him. "Go ahead. Write it, Wally. Make them squirm a little. Maybe they *won't* do any of it, but they've got to at least say they're sorry."

Wally finished the note.

"How do we sign it?" Josh wondered.

"How did they sign theirs?" asked Jake.

"The Malloy Musketeers," said Wally.

Jake thought a minute. "The Hatford Hooligans," he decided, and they all signed their names.

"Who's going to deliver it?" asked Josh. "Peter?"

"Are you crazy?" said Jake. "They'll simply kidnap Peter!"

"We'll *all* deliver it!" said Josh. "All four of us will go over there together. Caroline can't escape, don't worry."

The boys looked toward the toolshed again.

"Hey, Caroline!" Wally called.

No answer.

"Hey, Crazie!" called Josh.

Still no answer.

"Maybe she dug her way out," said Peter.

The boys started across the lawn. Wally was feeling a little uneasy. The sun was shining right on the metal shed, and he knew how hot it got in the summertime. It wasn't summer any longer, but it was still warm. Maybe she had overheated. Maybe she was dead!

"Listen, guys, I don't know if we ought to keep

her in there," he said. "That shed gets awfully hot in the afternoons."

"Did *we* put her there?" Jake said. "It was her idea. She would have stayed all day, I'll bet, if we hadn't found her. All we did was put a padlock on the door."

"But suppose she got sick or something?" Wally said. "Man, we'd really catch it."

They stopped outside the shed.

"Hey, Caroline," Josh said again. "Are you dead?"

"Oh, she's just playing possum to make you open the door," said Jake.

"Remember that hot day in August when our old dog got distemper?" Wally reminded them. They looked at each other uneasily.

"Hey, Caroline, you want some water?" Wally called.

No answer. No sound at all.

Jake dialed the combination on the lock and opened the door, just a little.

They all stepped backward. Caroline was sitting on the floor of the shed, her eyes closed. White foam was oozing out one corner of her mouth.

"What's the matter with her?" asked Peter.

"I don't know," said Jake. "Hey, Caroline, come on out. You can go home now."

Caroline opened her eyes once, and they looked wild. Then they closed again.

"Jake . . . !" Wally said worriedly.

"Go on home, Caroline," Jake said.

The girl didn't move.

"What are we going to do?" asked Wally, and his heart began to pound.

"Forget the note," said Jake, and Wally knew he was worried too. "Go call her sisters, Wally, and tell them to come and get her. That Caroline's over here sick."

Wally made a beeline for the house, and went up the steps two at a time.

He quickly dialed the Malloys' number. What if the parents answered? What was he supposed to say? That Caroline was locked in the toolshed foaming at the mouth?

The phone rang five times before anyone answered.

"Hello?" It sounded like Eddie.

"Your sister's sick," said Wally.

There was a pause. "Who is this?" Eddie asked.

"Wally. Caroline's in our toolshed. You better come and get her."

"Yeah? What kind of a trick is this?" Eddie said. "I saw your folks drive away. You must think we're really stupid."

Wally's hand felt sweaty on the telephone. "Listen," he said again. "I mean it. She's foaming at the mouth."

"What?"

"We just unlocked the shed and I think she's got distemper. There's white stuff all over her lips."

"Hold on." It sounded as though Eddie had her hand over the receiver and was talking to somebody else. Then Beth came on the line.

"What's the matter with Caroline?" Beth asked.

"I already said! She's foaming at the mouth and acting weird, and you better come get her."

"How did she get in your shed?" asked Beth.

"She went there herself. We didn't put her there. She was spying on us."

"Then how did the shed get locked?"

"After we found her, we locked the door."

"Well, if you locked her in there and she's sick, you better call an ambulance," Beth said, and hung up.

Wally stared at the phone in his hand. Then slowly replaced the receiver and went out to the others on the back steps.

"Are they coming?" asked Jake.

Wally shook his head. "They said to call an ambulance."

"Hoo boy!" Josh whistled through his teeth. "We can't call an ambulance! Dad would be furious!"

"Yeah, but if something happened to her and we didn't, he'd kill us," Wally said.

The boys stared at each other. "You think we should try to carry her home ourselves?" Jake said.

"Let's try," said Wally.

They went back to the shed again. Caroline had

crawled behind the lawn mower now, and was making strange noises, half dog, half human.

"What's she doing?" asked Peter, eyes wide.

"Biting her own arm!" breathed Josh, and the boys retreated slowly to the back steps.

"What if she's rabid?" asked Wally.

"Don't be dumb."

"What if she *is*? What if a strange dog bit her before they left Ohio and nobody even knew it?"

Jake let out his breath. "Boy, I hope she leaves before Mom and Dad get home." He hunched his shoulders. "Look," he said to Wally. "Go call Beth and Eddie again, and tell them we'll make a deal. They come and get Caroline, and we'll call off the war for good. No more tricks again ever."

Wally went back inside and called the Malloys. Eddie answered again.

"Listen," he began. It was all he could think of to say. "Come over and get Caroline, and we'll call off the war for good. No more tricks again ever."

"No deal," Eddie said, and the receiver clicked again.

Wally reported it to the others.

"They *have* to take her!" bleated Jake. "She's their *sister*! What kind of sisters are they if they won't even come and get someone who's rabid!"

"What time is it?" asked Josh.

Jake looked at his watch. "Almost two. Mom and Dad could be driving back any minute."

Wally's stomach seemed to turn upside down.

"It doesn't matter whether we took the padlock off or not," he said finally. "The fact is we *did* have the padlock on for a while, so that she couldn't get out if she'd wanted to. And she *was* in there for at least an hour. That might have been long enough to do it. We're responsible no matter what."

"I'm not touching her," said Josh.

"Me either," said Peter.

"*I'll* call the Malloys," Jake said, and his voice sounded a little shaky. Wally went back inside with him. Jake dialed.

This time the phone must have rung ten times before Eddie answered.

"Yes?" she said loudly, impatiently. Wally was standing three feet away and he could hear every word she said. "What is it *now*?"

"Look," Jake began.

"Look . . . listen. . . . Is that all you guys can say?"

"We'll make any kind of deal you want if you just come and get Caroline," Jake told her.

The silence this time must have lasted for ten whole seconds. To Wally it seemed forever.

"Any kind of deal we want?"

"Yeah. Just come and get her."

"Say, 'Please.' "

"Please," murmured Jake.

"Say, 'Pretty please.' "

Wally heard Jake swallow. "Pretty please," he said.

"Say, 'Pretty please from your faithful and obedient servant.'"

"Hey, listen. . . ."

"*Say* it!"

"Pretty please from your . . ."

There was the sound of a car pulling in the drive.

"The *folks* are home!" Jake said into the receiver. "Come and get her! Hurry!"

"Say the rest. . . ."

"Your faithful, obedient servant," Jake said, and hung up the phone. "I think I'm going to throw up," he said to Wally.

Fifteen

▼

Bamboozled

Caroline was beginning to wonder how much longer she had to roll around the floor of the shed with marshmallow on her lips before her sisters came after her.

It was entirely by accident that she had discovered the marshmallow foam. Once she found that the boys had padlocked the door, she had popped a marshmallow into her mouth for energy, then realized how thirsty she was. Sloshing the marshmallow sauce around in her mouth, she was thinking that if she ever had to play the part of a madwoman, she could use marshmallow foam. And it didn't take long to decide what to do when the boys came again to check on her. All she had to do to make *that* happen was be quiet.

Little snatches of conversation came from the steps across the yard. "They *have* to take her. . . ." "I'm not touching her. . . ." "We're responsible. . . ." Caroline decided that if she didn't need a drink of water so much, she could probably hold out for another couple of hours.

The next thing she heard was the sound of a car pulling in the drive, but even before it stopped, the back door slammed and she heard Jake say quickly, "They're coming! Beth and Eddie are on the way."

What should she do now, she wondered. This could be her grandest performance yet. Should she go on pretending to be rabid, so that Beth and Eddie had to carry her home? Or should she wait until her sisters opened the door of the shed, and then they could all have a big laugh together? Or maybe she could make a grand entrance now, by herself, and—

"*Three* bushels of apples," she heard Mrs. Hatford saying. "They were the best I've seen in a long, long time. And I don't want to hear any complaining. You didn't want to help pick them, so you can certainly help peel them. Won't do you one bit of harm."

She had better wait until the parents had gone inside, Caroline thought. Mrs. Hatford might figure out right away what was on her lips, and she didn't want to reveal the joke until Beth and Eddie were there.

The back door slammed as Mr. and Mrs. Hatford went inside. Three minutes later there came the crunch of footsteps on the gravel drive, and the sound of girls' low voices. Caroline could hardly keep from laughing out loud, and when Eddie opened the door of the shed at last, Caroline was sitting on the floor grinning, a marshmallow perched on her head.

The three burst out laughing.

"I *told* you it was probably marshmallow," said Beth. "I *knew* she couldn't get that sick in two hours."

"Oh, Eddie," Caroline shrieked happily. "It was my best performance. They thought I was rabid! They thought I was mad! They were even afraid to touch me."

"Did you know they called three times trying to get us to come and get you?" Beth giggled.

"And you know what we made them say?" asked Eddie. "Your faithful, obedient servant."

The girls howled.

They turned and started back across the yard. Josh and Jake were still on the steps with Peter, their faces pink with embarrassment.

Just then the back door opened and out stepped Mrs. Hatford, carrying a huge pan of apples. Mr. Hatford was behind her, carrying one of the bushels.

"Hello, girls," she called cheerfully.

Caroline, Beth, and Eddie stopped dead in their tracks.

"Wally just told me you were coming," Mrs. Hatford went on. "How nice of you to volunteer! I think we could do them right here in the yard, don't you?"

The girls stared in astonishment, then gave a low moan as Wally, paring knives in hand, came down the back steps with a smile wide as Christmas.

About the Author

Readers of Phyllis Reynolds Naylor's boys-versus-girls books often want to know who's finally going to win the war. Well, says Naylor, she herself is a girl, but she raised two sons, so she knows how boys feel too. Readers will just have to wait to see what the Hatfords and the Malloys have in mind.

The town of Buckman in the stories is really Buckhannon, West Virginia, where Naylor's husband spent most of his growing-up years.

Phyllis Reynolds Naylor is the author of more than a hundred books, including the Newbery Award-winning *Shiloh* and the other two books in the Shiloh trilogy, *Shiloh Season* and *Saving Shiloh*. She and her husband live in Bethesda, Maryland. They are the parents of two grown sons and have three grandchildren.